THE VIKING STUDENT WORLD ATLAS

VIKING KESTREL

VIKING KESTREL
Viking Penguin Inc., 40 West 23rd Street New York, New York 10010

Copyright © John Bartholomew & Son Limited, 1986
All rights reserved

First published in Great Britain by John Bartholomew & Son Limited, 1985
as The Illustrated Reference Atlas of the World
Published in 1986 by Viking Penguin Inc.

Printed in Great Britain

Library of Congress Catalog Card No: 85-40954
(CIP data available)

Cover photograph courtesy of NASA

Acknowledgements
The Publishers acknowledge with thanks the assistance of the following in preparing this publication:
Dr Walter Stephen
Senior Adviser, Curriculum, Dean Education Centre, Edinburgh
Alister Hendrie
Assistant Headteacher, Portobello High School, Edinburgh
Andrew Grant
Principal Teacher, Geography, Wester Hailes Education Centre, Edinburgh
Stephen Hamilton
Principal Teacher, Geography, Broughton High School, Edinburgh

The Publishers are grateful to the following for providing the photographs used in this atlas:
(picture number(s) shown in italics)
Travel Photo International: pages 6-7, savanna, rain forest, prairie, northern forest; page 12, *7*;
page 21, *2*; page 27, *11*; page 28, *4, 5, 13, 14*; page 30, *7*; page 31, *2*; page 46, *3, 4*; page 54, *3, 4*
Photographers' Library: pages 6-7, scrub *Chris Knaggs photograph*, desert *Oliver Martel photograph*
page 10, *8 Clive Sawyer photograph*; page 26, *8 Ian Wright photograph*
page 29, *9 Tom Hustler photograph*; page 30, *4 Robyn Beeche photograph*
Biofotos page 10, *5 Heather Angel photograph*; page 30, *6 Andrew Henley photograph*
page 31, *3 Soames Summerhays photograph*
The Photo Source page 12, *10*; page 21, *4*; page 26, *7*
Wade Cooper Associates, Edinburgh page 28, *12*; page 29, *10*; page 46, *1*
Pictor International page 26, *6*; page 46, *2*
B. and C. Alexander pages 6-7, tundra
Bruce Coleman Ltd page 54, *6 WWF/Eugen Schuhmacher photograph*
Mepha page 21, *1 C. Osborne photograph*
Michael Scott pages 6-7, woodland and grass
Yorkshire and Humberside Tourist Board page 11, *2*

CONTENTS

INTRODUCTION

This atlas for the 8-13 age group bridges the gap between pictorial atlases intended for young children and the much more complex atlases published for adults. The political and physical maps are just like those in a 'proper' atlas, drawn to scale with layer colouring to show how high the land is. But they have been simplified to make it easy to find country names, borders, main towns and physical features such as rivers and mountains. Where there is an English version of a place name, it is given first followed by the local language version.

The layout of the atlas is easy to follow. Pages 4 and 5 show how flat, two-dimensional maps can be drawn to show the rounded, three-dimensional world, and explain the idea of scale as it relates to maps. The map of world environments on pages 6 and 7 shows the 8 different climatic areas found in the world, with descriptions of the types of vegetation to be seen in each area. The key map and key to symbols on pages 8 and 9 will help in understanding and using the maps. Each of the boxes on the key map outlines an area covered by a particular map in the atlas. The number of the page where the map can be found is given in the inside top right-hand corner of each box. The symbols used on the maps are also explained, with examples.

The main part of the atlas, pages 10-58, is divided into continental sections – Europe, Africa, etc. Each section begins with a political map naming the countries included. Gazetteers for some of the larger countries show their flags and list their size, population, capital, language and currency. A 'Did you know that?' panel gives details of more unusual and surprising facts and places, some of which are illustrated. All the facts are keyed with numbers to their location on the political map. The number of each fact, the number of its picture (if there is one) and its number on the map are all the same. E.g. Fact **4** is illustrated in picture **4** and **4** on the map shows where in the world it can be found. There are also maps showing population distribution, and the type of natural vegetation and products of each part of the continent. A location globe shows exactly where the area covered in the political map is, in relation to the rest of the world. Physical maps covering each part of the continent in more detail make up the rest of the continental section. On every map spread there is another location globe which provides a quick answer to the question 'Where in the world is that?'.

The last six pages of the atlas contain an index to many of the places and geographical features shown on the maps. Each entry gives the name of the place, what it is (island, region etc), the name of the country or part of the world where it can be found, and a page number and grid reference. So the entry: London *Eng* **16C3**, refers to London, England which can be found on the map on page 16, in the area located by running a finger down from the letter C at the top of the page and in from the number 3 at the side of the page.

SCALE

Scale means how big one thing is, compared to another. For example, a model car can be a scale model of a real car. Drawing something 'to scale' is a way of making a picture or map of something big fit on to a small piece of paper. The important fact about a scale model or scale drawing is that from it, you can find out the size of the real thing – whether it is a car or a country. All you need to know is the scale that was used. The scale of a scale drawing will be shown on the scale bar beside it. It might look like this:

A short length (for example 1 cm) on the scale bar will stand for a longer one (for example 1 m) in the real world. By measuring the drawing and converting your measurements using the scale bar, you know the size of the real thing.

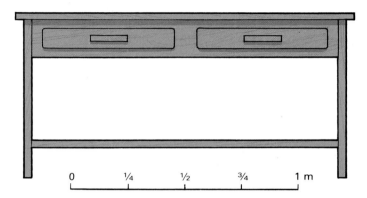

The picture shows a scale drawing of a table. Measure it to find out how long and high the real table was (use the scale bar!).

As you make scale drawings of bigger and bigger things, the short length on the scale bar has to stand for longer and longer lengths in the real world. Otherwise the drawings would not fit on to pieces of paper that could be held easily. Look at the plan of the classroom. What scale is it drawn to? How long are the walls of the real classroom?

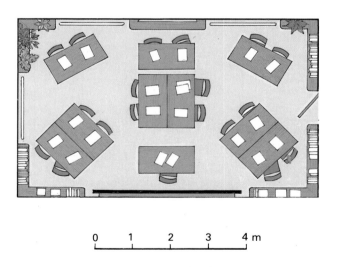

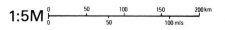

Cartographers (people who draw maps) make scale drawings of very big things – places and countries. So a small length on a map (for example 1 cm) has to stand for a very large one in real life (for example 1 km (100 000 cm) or 50 km (5 000 000 cm)). These examples could be written 1:100 000 or 1:5M (M stands for 'million'). When a scale is written like this, it is called a Representative Fraction (RF for short). Most maps have a scale bar as well as an RF. So if two places on a map are 6 cm apart and at the top of the page you see this:

1:5M 0 50 100 150 200 km
0 50 100 mls

you can work out that the real places are 300 km apart.

All the maps in this atlas have an RF and scale bar at the top of the page. The scale of the maps varies, depending on the size of the area each has to show.

MAP PROJECTIONS

People who make flat maps have one big problem: the world is spherical (like an orange). If you peel the skin off an orange

you will discover that you cannot make the pieces of skin lie flat unless you push them out of shape. In the same way, if map makers want to draw a flat map, they have to change the shapes or sizes (or both) of the countries on the surface of the earth. The only kind of map without these distortions (as the changes in shape and size are called) is a globe – a spherical map (right).

Over the centuries, many different ways of making flat maps of the earth have been discovered. They are called **Map Projections**. A projector makes an image on a screen by shining a light through a piece of film. Map makers pretended to shine a light through from the inside of the world and drew the outlines of countries as they would look on a flat surface. This type of map is called an **Azimuthal Projection**.

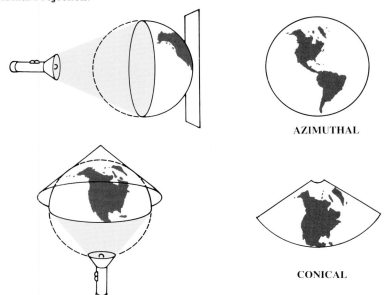

AZIMUTHAL

CONICAL

By 'shining a light' through different parts of the world (the top, the sides and so on) different maps could be drawn. The next step was to change the shape of the 'screen' onto which the outlines of countries were projected. Some map makers used a cone shape. Their maps are called **Conical Projections**. Others used a cylinder shape, as if a piece of paper had been wrapped round the world. A map made like this is called a **Cylindrical Projection**. Other ways of drawing maps were developed, which did not use this idea of 'shining a light', but they are all called 'projections' from the first way of drawing them.

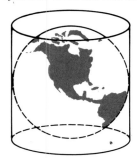 

CYLINDRICAL

All projections distort land and sea areas and their positions in different ways. Map makers choose the projection they want to use depending on what the map is for. They consider things like relative sizes of areas, shapes of areas, directions and distances. Look at the box on the right, showing Australia drawn using three different projections (there are many more than that); see how different the shape of the country is.

THREE PROJECTIONS OF AUSTRALIA

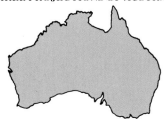

INTERRUPTED SINUSOIDAL
Distances are accurate along all parallels of latitude and on each centre meridian.

PETERS PROJECTION
Modified Mercator projection (cylindrical) which tries to show the sizes of different countries in proportion to each other. Often used for maps showing the inequality of wealth distribution in proportion to country size and population.

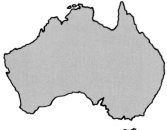

MERCATOR
Distances are accurate but land areas are distorted; traditionally used for navigation; the most popular projection in the past for world maps.

6 WORLD MAP OF THE ENVIRONMENT

The world can be divided into 8 broad 'climatic zones' (these are areas with a particular sort of weather). The natural types of plants and animals found in each zone are different and depend on the weather the zone has. This map shows which parts of the world are in each zone. The colour of the strip at the top of each zone description (for example, Desert, Rainforest) is the same as the colour used for the zone on the big map. The little map beside each zone description pinpoints where that type of habitat is found in the world. (For example, the Desert strip is orange/yellow. The little sketch map shows you where on the big map to look for this colour. You will find this colour in the north of Africa, the west of North America and in parts of Asia and Australia. All these places have deserts. The description tells you what the natural countryside looks like and what plants and animals live there.)

SCRUB OR MEDITERRANEAN

Areas of long, hot, dry summers and short, warm winters. The land used to be covered with trees, but man cleared it for crops and grazed his animals on it. Now there is evergreen scrub – vines and olive trees.

TUNDRA OR MOUNTAIN

Polar areas which are usually frozen over. During the short summers the top layer of soil thaws, creating vast marshes. Compact, wind-resistant plants and lichens and mosses are found here. Animals include lemmings and reindeer.

NORTHERN FOREST (TAIGA)

Forests of conifers growing over a large area. Winters are very cold and long. Summers are short. Trees include spruce and fir. Animals found here include beavers, squirrels and red deer.

WOODLAND AND GRASS

Temperate areas (where the weather is seldom very cold or very hot). Deciduous trees (which lose their leaves in winter) grow in the woodlands. They include oak, beech and maple. Man uses these areas most of all, for farming, building towns and villages, and industry.

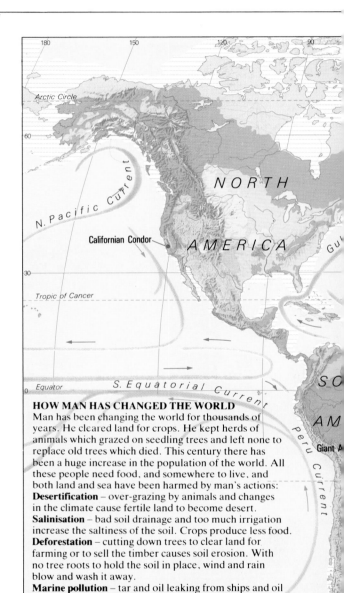

HOW MAN HAS CHANGED THE WORLD
Man has been changing the world for thousands of years. He cleared land for crops. He kept herds of animals which grazed on seedling trees and left none to replace old trees which died. This century there has been a huge increase in the population of the world. All these people need food, and somewhere to live, and both land and sea have been harmed by man's actions:
Desertification – over-grazing by animals and changes in the climate cause fertile land to become desert.
Salinisation – bad soil drainage and too much irrigation increase the saltiness of the soil. Crops produce less food.
Deforestation – cutting down trees to clear land for farming or to sell the timber causes soil erosion. With no tree roots to hold the soil in place, wind and rain blow and wash it away.
Marine pollution – tar and oil leaking from ships and oil drilling rigs into enclosed seas (like the Mediterranean) harm their plants and animals.

GRASSLAND

Hot summers, cold winters and moderate rainfall. Huge area of grassland and 'black' (very fertile) soils. Grain crops grow well, and so does rich pasture for beef cattle. Names for this kind of grassland include steppe, veld, pampas and prairie.

SAVANNA

Tall grasses with thick stems, and flat-topped thorny trees grow here. Animals grazing here include giraffes and zebras. There is a short rainy season. Often it does not rain for a long time (a drought). Fires burn the dried out plants but they have adapted to survive this and grow again.

DESERT

These areas have bare mountains, rocky wastes and sand dunes. Plants (wiry grass, thorn bushes and cacti) and animals (lizards and camels) must be well adapted to survive very high temperatures and little water. It may rain only once in several years.

North Pole

Arctic Circle

N. Atlantic Drift

European Bison

N. Atlantic Drift

EUROPE

Abruzzo Brown Bear

POLLUTION

Monk Seal

Przewalski's Horse

ASIA

Desertification

Giant Panda

Kuro-Shio

AFRICA

Bengal Tiger

DESERTIFICATION

Arabian Oryx
Hunted by man

(July)

Salinisation

Asiatic Lion
Last remnant

Orang-utan
Only great ape
outside C.Africa

N. Equatorial Current

DEFORESTATION

Monsoon Drift

(July)

(July)

(Jan)

DEFORESTATION

DEFORESTATION

Guinea Current

(July)

Indian Counter Current

Mountain Gorilla

Equatorial Current (Jan)

Equatorial Current

(July)

Woolly Spider Monkey

Benguela Current

Indris
Largest surviving lemur

Numbat
Marsupial

(Jan)

Brazil Current

AUSTRALIA

Tropic of Capricorn

Giant Anteater

30

Parma Wallaby
Last remnant

West · Wind · Drift

Takahe
Flightless bird

- Endangered wildlife
- Continental shelf
- Ice shelf

Ocean Circulation
- Surface currents-warm
- Surface currents-cold

South Pole

Antarctic Circle

RAINFOREST

Hot and wet, with no real winter or summer. Trees with thick foliage, climbing plants, monkeys and tigers are found here. There are five 'layers' of plants in a rainforest: the high trees, the tree canopy, the open canopy, shrubs and ground plants.

8 KEY MAP

This map shows you which part of the world is shown in each of the regional maps in this atlas. The area of each regional map is outlined in black (physical maps) or red (political maps). In the top right hand corner of each map box is a number (or two numbers) e.g. 16, 38-39. This is the number of the page or pages where you will find a map of the area within the black, or red-outlined box. The list below gives the name of each map.

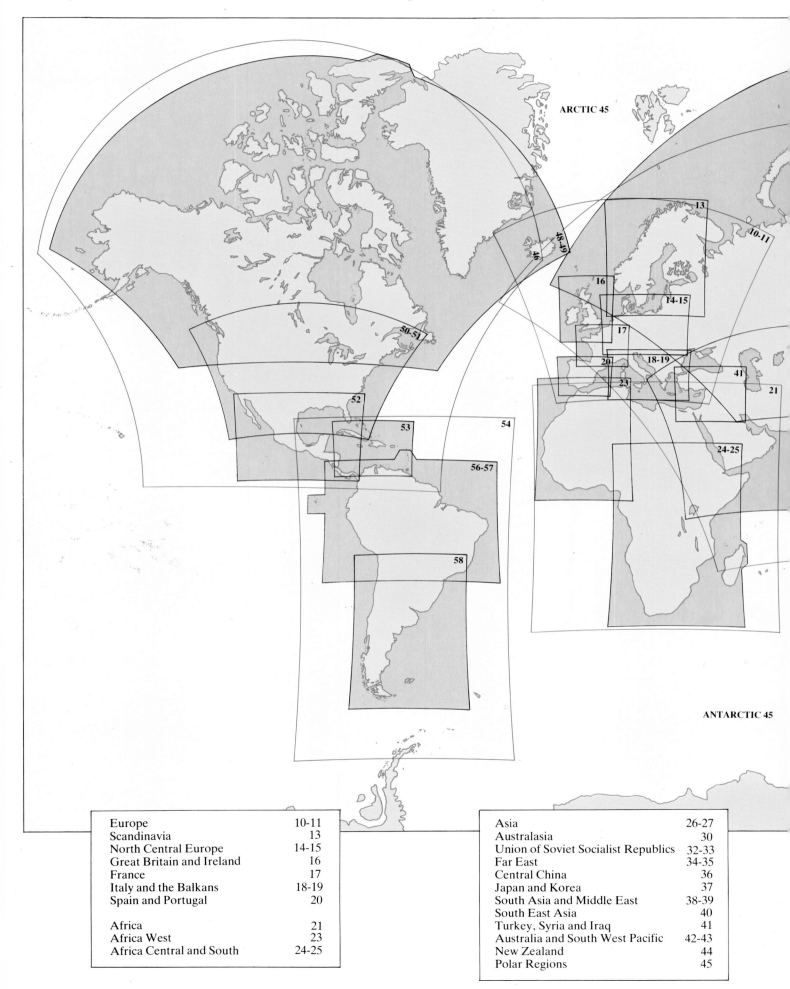

ARCTIC 45

13
10-11
48-49
46
50-51
16
14-15
17
20
18-19
41
23
21
52
24-25
53
54
56-57
58

ANTARCTIC 45

LETTERING STYLES

CANADA	Independent Nation
FLORIDA	State, Province or Autonomous Region
Gibraltar (U.K.)	Sovereignty of Dependent Territory
Lothian	Administrative Area
LANGUEDOC	Historic Region
Loire *Vosges*	Physical Feature or Physical Region

This panel explains the different lettering styles, the main symbols and the height and depth colours used on the reference maps in this atlas.

TOWNS AND CITIES

Square symbols mark capital cities — *Population*

■	●	**New York**	over 5 000 000
■	●	**Montréal**	over 1 000 000
□	○	Ottawa	over 500 000
▪	•	Québec	over 100 000
▫	◦	St John's	over 50 000

 Built-up-area

LAKE FEATURES

	Freshwater
	Saltwater
	Seasonal
	Salt Pan

OTHER FEATURES

	River
	Seasonal River
≍	Pass, Gorge
	Dam, Barrage
	Waterfall, Rapid
	Aqueduct
	Reef
▲ 4231	Summit, Peak

BOUNDARIES

	International
	International under Dispute
	Cease Fire Line
	Autonomous or State
	Administrative
	Maritime (National)
	International Date Line

LANDSCAPE FEATURES

	Glacier, Ice Cap
	Marsh, Swamp
	Sand Desert, Dunes

Height

6000m
5000m
4000m
3000m
2000m
1000m
500m
200m

0   0   Sea Level

200m
2000m
4000m
6000m
8000m

Depth

Map index numbers: 32-33, 26-27, 37, 34-35, 36, 38-39, 40, 30, 42-43, 44

1:15M

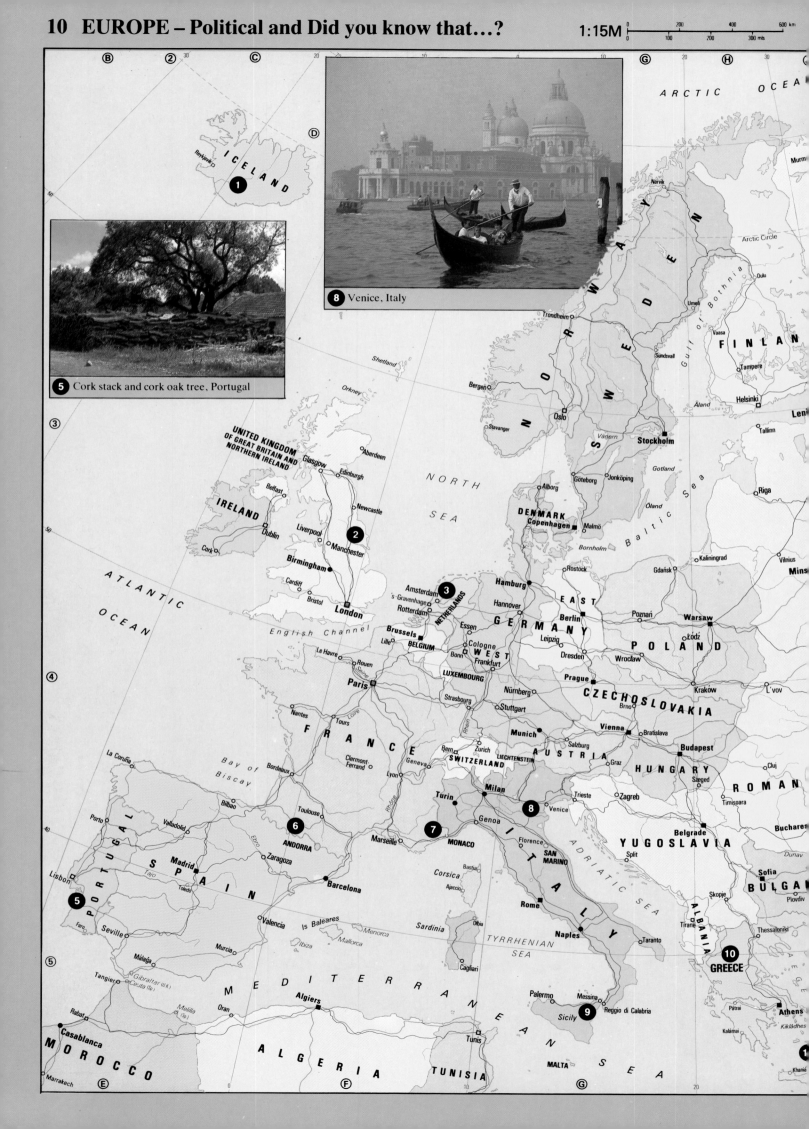

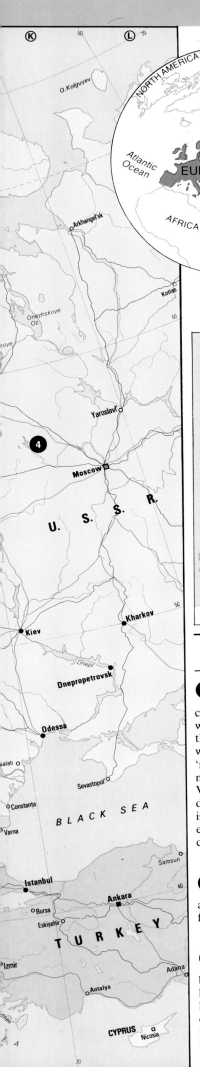

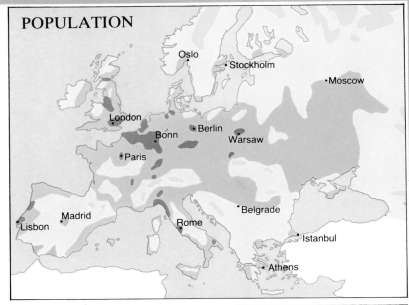

POPULATION

Oslo · Stockholm · Moscow

London · Bonn · Berlin · Warsaw

Paris

Madrid · Belgrade · Rome · Istanbul

Lisbon · Athens

	over 500 persons per km²
	100-500 persons per km²
	5-100 persons per km²
	under 5 persons per km²

NATURAL VEGETATION/ PRODUCTS

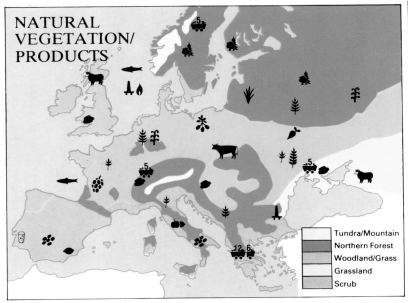

Tundra/Mountain
Northern Forest
Woodland/Grass
Grassland
Scrub

	Cattle		Oil
	Sheep		Coal
	Fish		Gas
	Fruit		Oats
	Citrus fruit		Wheat
	Grapes		Maize
	Yams		Rye
	Sugar beet		Barley
	Potatoes	5	Iron
	Timber	6	Lead
	Cork	12	Zinc

DID YOU KNOW THAT ...?

1 In Iceland, ice and fire exist side by side! Many active volcanoes and geysers (hot springs which shoot a column of water into the air at intervals) can be seen, while glaciers (continually moving 'rivers' of ice) and ice sheets cover much of the land. One volcano – Vatnajokull – is particularly dangerous for an unusual reason: it is underneath a glacier and when it erupts, the ice melts very quickly, causing terrible floods.

2 The Humber Bridge, England, has the longest main span of any bridge in the world. It stretches for 1410 m (4626 feet).

3 More than a third of the land area of the Netherlands has been reclaimed from the sea! These lands (the *polders*) are below sea level and the sea is kept out by dykes. Drainage ditches divide the fertile fields. The water from them is pumped into canals and rivers, then out to sea.

4 The longest river in Europe is the Volga, which runs for 3690 km (2293 miles) from the forests north west of Moscow all the way to the Caspian Sea.

5 Portugal is an important source of cork, which is actually the bark of a tree! The cork oak produces cork bark up to 15 cm (6 inches) thick and this is stripped off the trees every 10 to 15 years. Cork oaks grow throughout the western and central Mediterranean region.

6 The Pierre Saint Martin Cavern in the Pyrenees mountains, France, is the deepest cave system yet discovered in the world. It goes 1330 m (4364 feet) into the heart of the mountains.

7 The principality of Monaco is one of the most crowded countries in the world: 28 000 people live on 1.9 sq km (467 acres) of land! By contrast, most of Scandinavia has fewer than 40 people per square kilometre!

8 Venice, Italy, is built on no less than 118 islands! Instead of roads, there are canals, and boats are used for transport. Venice is sinking at a rate of 12 inches each century. Some of the reasons for this include water being extracted from wells, and the compression of the mud on the floor of the lagoon.

9 Mount Etna, Sicily, is the highest volcano in Europe (about 3323 m, 10 902 ft) and is still very active. Despite this, many people live on its lower slopes! This is because the soil there is very fertile and grows good produce.

2 The Humber Bridge, England

AUSTRIA

Area: 83 848 sq km
(32 374 sq miles)
Population: 7 600 000
Capital: Vienna
Language: German
Currency: Schilling

BELGIUM

Area: 30 512 sq km
(11 781 sq miles)
Population: 9 900 000
Capital: Brussels
Languages: Flemish, French
Currency: Belgian Franc

DENMARK

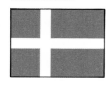

Area: 43 030 sq km
(16 614 sq miles)
Population: 5 100 000
Capital: Copenhagen
Language: Danish
Currency: Krone

EAST GERMANY

Area: 107 860 sq km
(41 645 miles)
Population: 16 700 000
Capital: Berlin (East)
Language: German
Currency: DDR Mark

FRANCE

Area: 551 000 sq km
(212 741 sq miles)
Population: 54 800 000
Capital: Paris
Language: French
Currency: Franc

GREECE

Area: 131 955 sq km
(50 948 sq miles)
Population: 10 000 000
Capital: Athens
Language: Greek
Currency: Drachma

IRELAND

Area: 70 282 sq km
(27 136 sq miles)
Population: 3 600 000
Capital: Dublin
Languages: Irish (Gaelic),
English
Currency: Irish Pound
(Punt)

ITALY

Area: 301 245 sq km
(116 311 sq miles)
Population: 57 000 000
Capital: Rome
Language: Italian
Currency: Lira

NETHERLANDS

Area: 33 940 sq km
(13 104 sq miles)
Population: 14 400 000
Capital: The Hague
Language: Dutch
Currency: Guilder

POLAND

Area: 312 683 sq km
(120 727 sq miles)
Population: 36 900 000
Capital: Warsaw
Language: Polish
Currency: Zloty

PORTUGAL

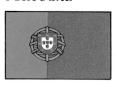

Area: 91 671 sq km
(35 394 sq miles)
Population: 10 100 000
Capital: Lisbon
Language: Portuguese
Currency: Escudo

SPAIN

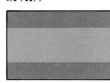

Area: 504 745 sq km
(194 882 sq miles)
Population: 38 400 000
Capital: Madrid
Language: Spanish
Currency: Peseta

UNITED KINGDOM

Area: 244 104 sq km
(94 249 sq miles)
Population: 56 000 000
Capital: London
Language: English
Currency: Pound Sterling

WEST GERMANY

Area: 248 528 sq km
(95 957 sq miles)
Population: 61 400 000
Capital: Bonn
Language: German
Currency: Deutschmark

YUGOSLAVIA

Area: 255 803 sq km
(98 766 sq miles)
Population: 23 000 000
Capital: Belgrade
Languages: Serbo-Croatian,
Macedonian, Slovenian
Currency: Dinar

10 Monasteries on rock pillars, Greece

10 Near Kalabaka, Greece, are a group of monasteries built for monks with no fear of heights. They are perched on top of pillars of rock, called meteora, 300 m (1 000 ft) high! The only way up was by ladders or baskets slung on the end of ropes. Now stairways have been constructed so that tourists can visit the buildings.

11 The island of Santorini (Thira) in Greece is the site of the world's largest natural disaster. About 1500 BC this volcanic island erupted leaving a *caldera* (hollow basin shape where the top of the volcano had been) about 13 km (8 miles) across. Many people believe that the destruction of this island is the origin of the story of Atlantis. The people of Atlantis are mentioned by the Greek writer Plato. Crime and corruption spread throughout their island as they became wealthier, until finally the Athenians conquered them. Later the island disappeared into the sea in a single day and night.

7 Monte Carlo, Monaco

1:7.5M

100   200   300 km
50   100   150 mls

ICELAND

Arctic Circle
25W   20   15

Akureyri

Vatnajökull

Reykjavik

the same scale

Færøerne (Den)

Tórshavn

Arctic Circle

7W   5

N O R W E G I A N   S E A

ARCTIC OCEAN

BARENTS SEA

Lofoten Vesterålen

Vestfjorden

Narvik

Bodø

Murmansk

Kol'skiy Poluostrov

Ivalo

L a p p l a n d

Gällivare

Kemijärvi

Luleå

Oulu

Karel'skaya A.S.S.R.

Trondheimfj.

Trondheim

Östersund

Gulf of Bothnia

Vaasa

FINLAND

Sundsvall

Glittertind 2470

Songnefjorden

Tampere

Ladozhskoye Ozero

Bergen

Hardangerfj.

Turku

Helsinki (Helsingfors)

Leningrad

Gulf of Finland

Oslo

Uppsala

Tallinn

Stavanger

Stockholm

ESTONSKAYA S.S.R.

ROSSIYSKAYA S.F.S.R.

Vänern

Norrköping

Gulf of Riga

Kristiansand

Gotland

Riga LATVIYSKAYA S.S.R.

Skagerrak

Göteborg   Jönköping

Ålborg

Kattegat

LITOVSKAYA S.S.R.

North

Århus Helsingborg

DENMARK

Copenhagen (København)

Sea Esbjerg

Odense

Malmö

Bornholm (Den.)

B A L T I C   S E A

Gulf of Gdańsk

Kaliningrad

Kiel

Rostock

Gdańsk

Wilhelmshaven

Hamburg

Bremen

WEST   **EAST**

Elbe

POLAND

GERMANY

Hannover

Berlin

Poznań

Warsaw (Warszawa)

Ⓐ Ⓑ Ⓒ

① ②

55

Göteborg ● Jönköping

Ⓐlborg ●

S W E D E N

Kattegat

D E N · M A R K

Jutland

Å rhus ●

Helsingborg ●

(Jylland)

Copenhagen
(København) ■

Esbjerg ○

Odense ○

Malmö ●

Sjælland

Fyn

Lolland

B A L T

B

N O R T H

S E A

SCHLESWIG-HOLSTEIN

Elbe

Hamburg ■

Elbe

② ○ Bremen

② **Amsterdam** ●

N I E D E R S A C H S E N

E A S T

Oder
(Odra)

The Hague
('s-Gravenhage) □

Hannover ○

Berlin ■

Rotterdam ●

G E R M A N Y

Mass

Rhein

NORDHREIN-

Lippe

Zeebrugge ○

Duisburg ○ ○Dortmund

Antwerp ●

Essen

Leipzig ○

Dunkerque ○

Schelde

Düsseldorf
WESTFALEN

Ruhr

Brussels
(Brüssel/
Bruxelles) ■

Cologne
(Köln) ●

Dresden ○ *Elbe*

Wro
(Bre

Lille ●

Bonn ○

50

Ardennes

H E S S E N

B E L G I U M

W E S T

LUXEM
BOURG

Mosel

Frankfurt ○

□ Luxembourg

RHEINLAND
PFALZ

Prague ■
(Praha)

SAAR
LAND

C Z E

Reims ●

③

G E R M A N Y

Nürnberg ○

L O R R A I N E

B O U R G O G N E

C H A M P A G N E

F R A N C E

B A D E N

B A Y E R N

Č E S K É   Z E M Ě

Seine

Stuttgart ○

Danube

V o s g e s

A L S A C E

WÜRTTEMBURG

F R A N C H E - C O M T É

Saône

S c h w a r z w a l d

③ Dijon ●

Munich ●
(München)

Vienna
(Wien) ■

J u r a

Salzburg ●

Zürich ○

LIECHTEN
STEIN

Innsbruck ●

A U S T R I A

S t

Brenner
1370

Grossglockner
3798

Bern ■

□ Vaduz

Rhein

S W I T Z E R L A N D

P

L

Jungfrau
4158

2112 St Gotthard

Rhône

Geneva
(Genève) ●

Simplon
2009 △

Alpi Dolomitiche

Lyon ●

4807 ▲ Mt
Blanc

△ *Matterhorn*
4472

I T A L Y

Ljubljana ●

S A V O I E

④

45

D A U P H I N É

Grenoble ●

Rhône

Milan ●
(Milano)

Venice ○
(Venezia)

Zagreb ○

Turin ●
(Torino)

G. di
Venezia

YU

Ⓐ Ⓑ

5 10 15

SEA

Gulf of Riga

E

F

30

G

°Riga

Velikiye-Luki

1

L A T V I Y S K A Y A S. S. R.

Daugavpils •

R. S. F. S. R.

55

L I T O V S K A Y A

Smolensk •

S. S. R.

Dnepr

Gulf of
Gdańsk

R. S. F. S. R.

Vilnius •

Minsk

Gdynia

B E L O R U S S K A Y A

Białystok •

S. S. R.

Bobruysk •

2

L A N D

Dneprovskaya

Gomel •

Vistula (Wisła)

Dnepr

Warsaw
(Warszawa)

Brest

N i z m e n n o s t'

Łódź°

Wisła

Lublin •

U. S. S. R.

50

Kiyev

Dnepr

Oder

Chorzow •

°Kraków

°L'vov

U K R A I N S K A Y A

Pridneprovskaya Vozv.

Podol'skaya

R.

S.   S.'skaya   Vozv

S L O V A K I A

Dnestr

M O L D A V S K A Y A

3

SLOVENSKO

Košice •

Carpatii Orientali

Nyíregyháza •

Baia Mare •

Budapest

N   G   A   R   Y

Cluj-Napoca •

Bacău •

S. S. R.

Odessa

Black Sea

Szeged •

Arad •

R   O   M   A   N   I   A

45

AVIA

Novi Sad •

Transylvanian Alps
(Mtii Carpatii Meridionali)

E

25

F

G

4

20

1:5M

0 50 100 150 200 km
0 50 100 mls

Ⓐ ① Ⓑ 5 Ⓒ 0 Ⓓ Ⓔ

10

60

Shetland

NORWAY

Orkney

C. Wrath

②

Outer Hebrides

The Minch

Inverness

NORTH

L. Ness

Aberdeen

SEA

SCOTLAND

Ben Nevis
1344 ▲

Dundee

Grampian Mts

L. Lomond

Glasgow *Edinburgh*

Clyde

55

Londonderry N. IRELAND *Stranraer*

Cheviots

L. Neagh *Larne*

Newcastle-upon-Tyne

Belfast

Pennines

Scafell Pike
972 ▲ *Middlesbrough*

Isle of Man

IRISH SEA

Leeds

Liverpool **Manchester**

Galway

Dublin
(Baile Átha Cliath) *Holyhead* **Sheffield**

Shannon

REP. OF
IRELAND

Wicklow Mts

▲ *1085*
Snowdon

The Wash

Norwich

③

Cambrian Mts

WALES **Birmingham** ENGLAND

NETHERLAND

The Hague
('s-Gravenhage)
Rotterdam

Cork

Bristol *Harwich*

Swansea

London

Cardiff *Thames* *Dover*

Zeebrugge

Antwerp BELGIUM

St George's Chan.

Southampton

Calais *Dunkerque* **Brussels**
(Brüssel/
Bruxelles)

Boulogne

ARTOIS **Lille**

Plymouth

50

Land's End

English Channel

PICARDIE

Cherbourg *Le Havre*

④

Channel Is
(U.K.)

NORMANDIE

10

Roscoff

■ **Paris**

FRANCE

Ⓑ 5 Ⓒ 0 Ⓓ

1:5M

| 50 | 100 | 150 | 200 km |
| 50 | | 100 mls |

EAST GERMANY

WEST GERMANY

Düsseldorf
Cologne (Köln)
Bonn
Frankfurt
Nürnberg
Stuttgart
Schwarzwald
Munich (München)
AUSTRIA
Innsbruck
LIECHTEN STEIN
Vaduz
Rhein
SWITZERLAND
Zürich
Bern
Geneva (Genève)
Mt Blanc 4807
SAVOIE
Grenoble
DAUPHINÉ
ITALY
Milan (Milano)
Turin (Torino)
Po
Genoa (Genova)
Bologna
Florence (Firenze)
Livorno
Elba
Bastia
CORSICA (CORSE)
Ligurian Sea
Nice
Monte Carlo
MONACO
Côte d'Azur
PROVENCE
Marseille
Golfe du Lion

ALSACE
Strasbourg
VOSGES
LORRAINE
Metz
LUXEMBOURG
Luxembourg
Ardennes
BELGIUM
Antwerp
Brussels (Brüssel/Bruxelles)
Dunkerque
Calais
Dover
Boulogne
ARTOIS
Lille
PICARDIE
Reims
CHAMPAGNE
JURA
FRANCHE-COMTÉ
Saône
Dijon
BOURGOGNE
Seine
NIVERNAIS
BERRY
ORLÉANAIS
Paris
Lyon
St-Étienne
AUVERGNE
Massif Central
Rhône
LANGUEDOC
GUYENNE
Toulouse
ROUSSILLON
ANDORRA
Pyrénées
GASCOGNE
NAVARRA
VASCONGADAS
Bilbao
SPAIN
ASTURIAS

ENGLAND
Plymouth
Portsmouth
Cherbourg
English Channel
Channel Is (U.K.)
Le Havre
Rouen
Seine
NORMANDIE
MAINE
ANJOU
Nantes
Tours
POITOU
LIMOUSIN
Limoges
Bordeaux
Roscoff
Brest
BRETAGNE
BAY OF BISCAY

1:5M

ITALY and THE BALKANS

Vienna (Wien)

Munich (München)
WEST GERMANY
Salzburg
Basel
Zürich
LIECHTENSTEIN
Vaduz
Innsbruck
AUSTRIA
Bern
SWITZERLAND
Brenner 1370
Graz
St Gotthard
2112
Geneva (Genève)
Simplon 2009
Matterhorn 4477
Alpi Dolomitiche
Ljubljana
Lyon
Mt St Bernard
Mt Blanc
Zagreb
FRANCE
Col du Mt Cenis 2803
Milan (Milano)
Verona
Venice (Venezia)
G. di Venezia
CROATIA
Turin (Torino)
Velebit
Genoa (Genova)
DALM
YU
Ligurian Sea
Florence (Firenze)
SAN MARINO
Ancona
MONACO
Livorno
Split (Spalato)
Marseille
ADRIATIC
Bastia
Elba
Pescara
Ajaccio
Civitavecchia
CORSICA (CORSE)
Rome (Roma)
Sassari
Olbia
Naples (Napoli)
Vesuvio 1277
SARDINIA (SARDEGNA)
TYRRHENIAN SEA
Cagliari
Cosenza
Stromboli
SICILY (SICILIA)
Messina
Palermo
Reggio di Calabria
MEDITERRANEAN
Etna 3323
Bone ('Annaba)
Syracuse (Siracusa)
Constantine
Tunis
ALGERIA
TUNISIA
MALTA

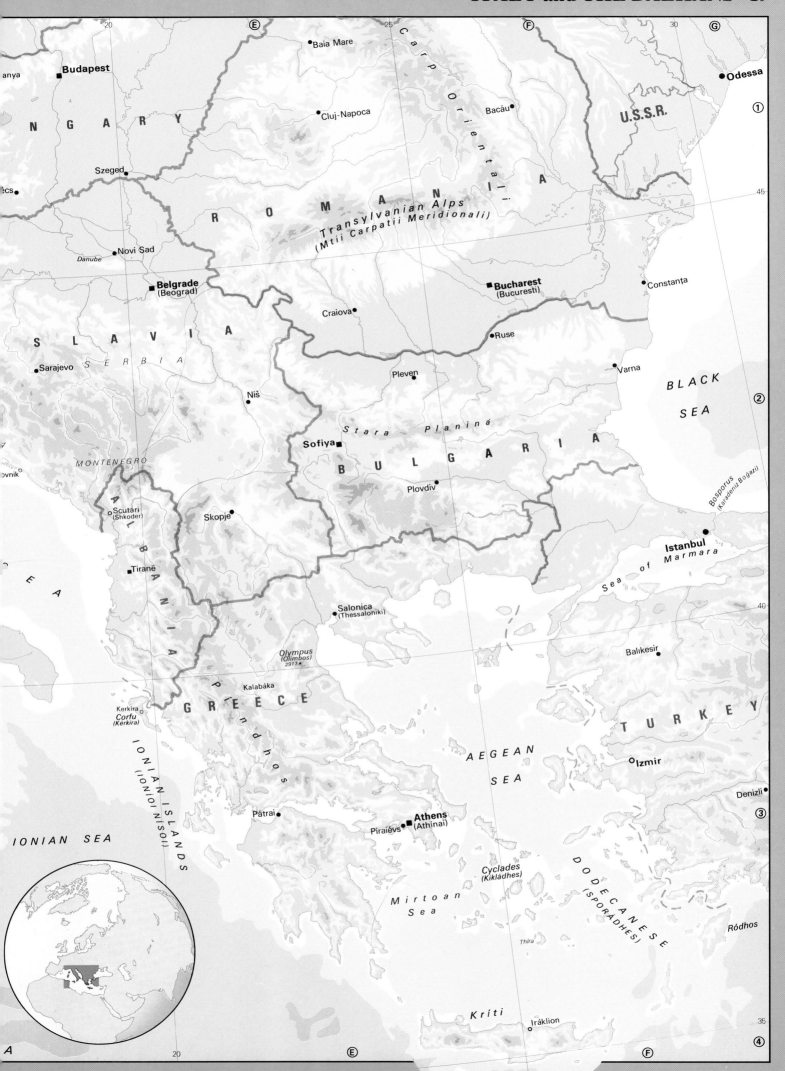

anya

Budapest

N G A R Y

Szeged

écs

Baia Mare

Cluj-Napoca

R O M A N I A

Transylvanian Alps
(Mtii Carpatii Meridionali)

Bacău

U.S.S.R.

Odessa

Novi Sad

Danube

Bucharest
(Bucureşti)

Constanţa

Belgrade
(Beograd)

Craiova

Ruse

S L A V I A

S E R B I A

Sarajevo

Niš

Pleven

Varna

BLACK

SEA

Stara   Planina

Sofiya

B U L G A R I A

MONTENEGRO

ovnik

Scutari
(Shkoder)

Skopje

Plovdiv

*Bosporus
(Karadeniz Boğazı)*

A

L

Tiranë

B
A
N
I
A

Istanbul

Sea of Marmara

Salonica
(Thessaloniki)

Olympus
(Olimbos)
2917

P
e
n
d
h
o
s

G R E E C E

Kalabáka

Balıkesir

T U R K E Y

E

A

Kerkira
Corfu
(Kérkira)

AEGEAN

SEA

Izmir

I
O
N
I
A
N

I
S
L
A
N
D
S

(IONIOI NISOI)

Denizli

Pátrai

Athens
(Athínai)

Piraiévs

IONIAN SEA

Cyclades
(Kikládhes)

D
O
D
E
C
A
N
E
S
E

(SPORADHES)

*Mirtoan
Sea*

Thíra

Ródhos

Krí ti

Iráklion

1:5M

0   50   100   150   200 km
0   50   100 mls

① 40 ②

Marseille○

Perpignan○

Costa Brava

Barcelona

Menorca

BALEARIC
ISLANDS
(ISLAS BALEARES)

Mallorca

Palma
de Mallorca

Algiers
(Alger)

Tarragona

ANDORRA
Andorra
La V.

Lérida

CATALUNA

Ibiza

Castellon de la P.

Valencia

Costa Blanca

Alicante

MEDITERRANEAN SEA

Oran○

FRANCE

Pyrénées
Pirineos

NAVARRA

ARAGON

Zaragoza

Burgos

○Bilbao

VASCONGADAS

Cantabrica

BAY OF BISCAY

Santander

Albacete

La Mancha

MURCIA

Murcia

Melilla (Sp.)

ESPAÑA

LA NUEVA

CASTILLA

Madrid

Granada

Sa Nevada

Costa de la Luz

Córdoba

Valladolid

CASTILLA LA VIEJA

Málaga

Costa del Sol

Oviedo

León

ASTURIAS

Cantabrica
Cordillera

DUERO

MORENA

Sierra

ANDALUCIA

Gibraltar (U.K.)

Str. of Gibraltar

GALICIA

EXTREMADURA

Badajoz

Seville
(Sevilla)

Cádiz

Tangier
(Tanger)

La Coruña○

PORTUGAL

TAGUS

Faro○

Oporto
(Porto)

Tagus (Tejo)

Lisbon
(Lisboa)

MOROCCO

① 40 ②

1:40M

400 800 1200 1600 km
400 800 mls

1 Bedouin tent in the Sahara

2 The River Nile, Aswan, Egypt

4 Mount Kilimanjaro, Tanzania

EUROPE
ASIA
AFRICA
Atlantic Ocean
Indian Ocean
SOUTH AMERICA

FINLAND
Helsinki
SWEDEN
Stockholm
Göteborg
Leningrad
Gor'kiy
Volga
Baltic Sea
Riga
Moscow
Minsk
Gdansk
Berlin
Warsaw
Kiev
Kharkov
Rostov
POLAND
Elbe
Wisla
Prague
Kraków
CZECHOSLOVAKIA
Vienna
AUSTRIA
Budapest
HUNGARY
Dnepr
Odessa
ROMANIA
YUGOSLAVIA
Belgrade
Bucharest
Danube
Sofia
BULGARIA
Adriatic Sea
Tirane
ALB.
Istanbul
Black Sea
Naples
Sicilia
GREECE
Athens
Kriti
Ankara
TURKEY
Tabriz
Tehrān
AFGHANISTAN
IRAN
PAK.

Madeira (Port.)
Tangier
Rabat
Fès
Oran
Algiers
Annaba
Tunis
TUNISIA
Constantine
Sfax
Mediterranean Sea
Tripoli
Benghāzi
Alexandria
Cairo
Port Said
Suez
Jerusalem
ISR.
Amman
JORDAN
Beirut
Damascus
SYRIA
LEB.
Nicosia
CYPRUS
Baghdād
IRAQ
Euphrates
Tigris
Basra
KUWAIT
Kuwait
BAHRAIN
Shirāz
The Gulf
QATAR
Abū Dhabi
UNITED ARAB EMIRATES
Muscat
OMAN
Marrakech
Casablanca
MOROCCO
Béchar
Islas Canarias (Sp.)
La'youn
Tindouf
In Salah
ALGERIA
Ghudamis
Sabha
LIBYA
Ghāt
Tropic of Cancer
Tamanrasset
'F'derik
MAURITANIA
Nouakchott
SAHARA
NIGER
EGYPT
Asyūt
Aswān
L. Nasser
Nile
SAUDI
ARABIA
Riyadh
Mecca
Red Sea
Port Sudan
Wadi Halfa
Atbara
Kassala
SOUTH YEMEN
San'ā
YEMEN
Aden
Gulf of Aden
Socotra (S.Y.)
Kuria Muria Is
St Louis
Sénégal
SENEGAL
Banjul
Dakar
GUINEA BISSAU
Conakry
Karkan
GUINEA
SIERRA LEONE
Freetown
Monrovia
Buchanan
LIBERIA
Tombouctou
MALI
Bamako
Niger
BURKINA (UPPER VOLTA)
Ouagadougou
Niamey
Agadez
L. Chad
Kano
Kaduna
Maiduguri
N'Djamena
CHAD
El Obeid
Omdurman
Khartoum
White Nile
Blue Nile
Asmara
Diredawa
Hargeysa
DJIBOUTI
Djibouti
Bobo Dioulasso
Tamale
BENIN
TOGO
Ilorin
Ibadan
Onitsha
NIGERIA
Ngaoundéré
CENTRAL AFRICAN REPUBLIC
Bambari
Wau
Juba
Jimma
Addis Ababa
ETHIOPIA
SOMALIA
Mogadishu
IVORY COAST
Bouaké
GHANA
Kumasi
Accra
Abidjan
Porto Novo
Lomé
Lagos
Port Harcourt
Douala
Yaoundé
CAMEROON
Bangui
Zaïre (Congo)
Kisangani
Gulu
L. Albert
UGANDA
Kampala
Entebbe
Goma
L. Edward
RWANDA
Kigali
BURUNDI
Bujumbura
Kigoma
L. Rudolf
KENYA
Nairobi
Kismaayo
Mombasa
INDIAN
OCEAN
Seychelles Arch.
Amirante Is
SEYCHELLES
Aldabra Is
Farquhar Is
Bioko
Principe
SÃO TOMÉ & PRINCIPE
São Tomé
Pagalu (Eq.G)
EQUATORIAL GUINEA
Malabo
Bata
Libreville
Lambaréné
GABON
CONGO
Brazzaville
Kinshasa
Matadi
Cabinda (Ang.)
Bandundu
Ilebo
Kananga
Mbuji-Mayi
Kindu
ZAIRE
Lake Victoria
Mwanza
Lake Tanganyika
Dodoma
Zanzibar
TANZANIA
Dar es Salaam
Arusha
Kalemié
Kamina
Lobito
Luanda
Moçâmedes
Malanje
Bié
ANGOLA
Lubumbashi
Ndola
Lusaka
ZAMBIA
Lichinga
Lake Nyasa
MALAWI
Lilongwe
Zomba
Nampula
MOZAMBIQUE
Mozambique Channel
Mayotte (Fr.)
COMOROS
Antseranana
Mahajanga
MADAGASCAR
Antananarivo
Toamasina
MAURITIUS
Réunion (Fr.)
Toliara
Tromelin (Fr.)
Kunene
Cubango
Okavango
SOUTH ATLANTIC OCEAN
Mbala
Mbeya
Mutare
Sofala
Ruvuma
Zambezi
L. Kariba
Harāre
ZIMBABWE
Gwelo
Bulawayo
Hwange
Maramba
Tsumeb
BOTSWANA
Serowe
Limpopo
Walvis Bay (S.A.)
Windhoek
NAMIBIA (S.W. AFRICA)
Keetmanshoop
Gaborone
Pretoria
Johannesburg
Mbabane
Maputo
SWAZILAND
Orange
SOUTH AFRICA
Kimberley
Bloemfontein
Maseru
LESOTHO
Durban
Cape Town
Port Elizabeth
East London
Tropic of Capricorn

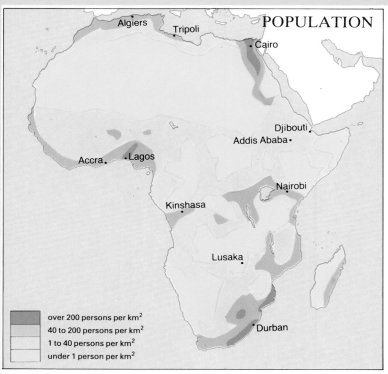

POPULATION

Algiers • Tripoli
• Cairo
Djibouti •
Addis Ababa •
Accra • Lagos
Nairobi •
Kinshasa •
Lusaka •
Durban •

over 200 persons per km²
40 to 200 persons per km²
1 to 40 persons per km²
under 1 person per km²

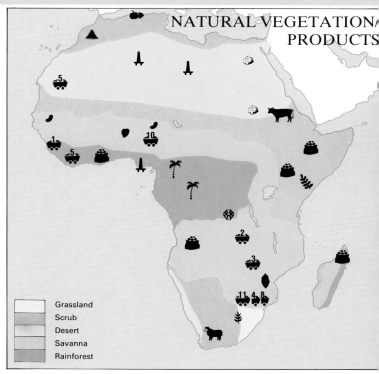

NATURAL VEGETATION
PRODUCTS

Grassland
Scrub
Desert
Savanna
Rainforest

DID YOU KNOW THAT …?

1 The largest desert in the world is the Sahara, but only about 30% of it is sand! The rest is rocky waste. People live mainly near oases, where the land is watered by springs rising to the surface and crops can be grown. The desert is very hot and dry, but there are a few plants and animals (like camels) specially adapted to these conditions.

2 The Nile is the longest river in the world and flows for 6650 km (4132 miles) through North Africa to the Mediterranean Sea.

The Nile used to flood its banks each year, but now the High Dam at Aswan controls the floods. When the dam was built, the temples of Abu Simbel (3000 years old) were moved to a higher site to stop them being flooded.

3 Some parts of Africa have had no rain, or very little, for several years. Food crops have failed and many people have died from malnutrition and starvation. A further problem has been wars, which have driven many people from their homes and fields. Even

if part of a country can grow food, it is difficult to move that food into areas where none can be grown. There are few lorries and, where people are at war, transporting food may be dangerous. Although western countries have sent food supplies, there is still not enough to feed the hundreds of thousands of people who are starving. Govern-

ments are trying to find ways of growing more food and distributing it more quickly.

4 Kilimanjaro (now renamed Uhuru, meaning 'freedom') is the highest mountain in Africa (5895 m; 19 340 feet) and its peaks are always covered in snow.

🐄	Cattle	🥜	Peanuts	▲	Phosphates	4	Gold
🐑	Sheep	🌴	Palm oil	✿	Maize	5	Iron
●	Cocoa	🌿	Tea	▣	Minerals	8	Platinum
▦	Coffee	◆	Tobacco	1	Bauxite	10	Tin
◌	Cotton	✦	Diamonds	2	Cobalt	11	Uranium
🍎	Fruit	⚒	Oil	3	Copper		

EGYPT

Area: 1 000 250 sq km (386 197 sq miles)
Population: 47 000 000
Capital: Cairo
Language: Arabic
Currency: Egyptian Pound

ETHIOPIA

Area: 1 221 918 sq km (471 783 sq miles)
Population: 32 000 000
Capital: Addis Ababa
Language: Amharic
Currency: Birr

KENYA

Area: 582 644 sq km (224 959 sq miles)
Population: 19 400 000
Capital: Nairobi
Languages: English, Swahili
Currency: Kenya Shilling

LIBYA

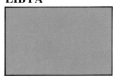

Area: 1 759 530 sq km (679 355 sq miles)
Population: 3 700 000
Capital: Tripoli
Language: Arabic
Currency: Libyan Dinar

NIGERIA

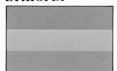

Area: 923 769 sq km (356 667 sq miles)
Population: 88 100 000
Capital: Lagos
Language: English
Currency: Naira

SOUTH AFRICA

Area: 1 221 038 sq km (471 443 sq miles)
Population: 31 700 000
Capital: Pretoria
Languages: Afrikaans, English
Currency: Rand

SUDAN

Area: 2 505 792 sq km (967 486 sq miles)
Population: 21 000 000
Capital: Khartoum
Language: Arabic
Currency: Sudanese Pound

ZAIRE

Area: 2 344 885 sq km (905 360 sq miles)
Population: 32 200 000
Capital: Kinshasa
Language: French
Currency: Zaire

1:15M

200	400	600 km
100	200	300 mls

Azores
(Açores)

Madeira
(Portugal)

Canary Islands
(Islas Canarias)
(Spain)

Lisbon
(Lisboa)
PORTUGAL

S P A I N

○Seville
(Sevilla)

Str. of
Gibraltar   Gibraltar *(U.K.)*
Tangiers   ○Ceuta *(Sp)*
(Tanger)   Tetouan
         Melilla
         (SP)

Casablanca   Rabat
(El-Dar-El-Beida)   Meknès

Marrakech

Haut   Atlas

M O R O C C O

Mostaganem
         El
Algiers   Asnam
(Alger)
         ●Batna

Tlemcen

○Laghouat

Skikda
(Philippeville)
Bône
(Annaba)
□Tunis

T U N I S I A

○Béchar

Grand Erg Occidental

Ouargla
El Golea

Grand erg Oriental

A L G E R I A

Tinfouchy

○La'youn

Western Sahara

Tropic of Cancer

Bir Meghrein

Erg Iguidi

El   Djouf

M A U R I T A N I A

S   A   H   A   R   A

Reggane○

○In Salah

Troudenni○

El   Khenachich

Tessalit○

Tamanrasset○

Tassili du Hoggar

akchott

El

M A L I

Niger

N I G E R

S E N E G A L

Mopti○

Tahoua○

Niamey●

Zinder○

Bamako●

B U R K I N A
(UPPER VOLTA)

○Sokoto

Kano●

sau□
NEA
SSAU

G U I N E A

Kankan○

Conakry●

S I E R R A
L E O N E
Freetown●

Bobo●
Dioulasso

Ouagadougou■

Bolgatanga●

Volta Noire

Black Volta

White Volta

Tamale○

Kaduna●

N I G E R I A

I V O R Y

C O A S T

Bouaké●

G H A N A

L.
Volta

T
O
G
O

B
E
N
I
N

Ibadan○

Benin●
City

Enugu●

L I B E R I A
Monrovia■

Kumasi●

Abidjan○

Accra□

Takoradi●

Lomé●

Porto Novo
■**Lagos**

Port●
Harcourt

C A M E R O O N

Bight of Benin

Moulths of the R. Niger

Douala●

■Yaoundé

Bight of
Biafra

EQUATORIAL
Bata□
GUINEA

CAPE VERDE

G U L F   O F   G U I N E A

S.TOME &
PRINCIPE

Libreville●

Equator

1:15M

200   400   600 km
100 200 300 mils

S A U D I   A R A B I A

Mecca

Jiddah

R E D   S E A

Y E M E N
Sanʿā
Al Hudaydah
(Hodeida)
Taʿizz

Aden
(Adan)

Gulf of Aden

Djibouti
DJIBOUTI

Berbera

Hargeysa

Harar

Port Sudan

Atbara

Kassala

Asmara

Gondar

Dessye

E T H I O P I A
Addis Ababa
Jimma
Yirga Alem

Khartoum
Omdurman
Wad Medani

Nile

El Obeid

S U D A N

En Nahud

Wadi Halfa

Nubian Desert

Malakal

Kenamuke Swamp

Wau

Juba

Gulu

Isiro

Belet Uen

S O M A L I

Mogadishu (Muqdisho)
Marka
Kismaayo

Mombasa

INDIAN

Equator

K E N Y A
Nairobi
▲5199 Mt. Kenya
Kilimanjaro ▲5895

Lake Rudolf

Masai Steppe

U G A N D A
Kampala

Lake Victoria

Kisangani (Stanleyville)

RWANDA
Kigali
BURUNDI
Bujumbura
Bukavu

Geneina

L I B Y A

Dépression du Mourdi

Tibesti

Plateau du Djado

Grand Erg de Bilma

N I G E R

Zinder

Kano

Maiduguri

N I G E R I A

Abéché

C H A D
N'Djamena (Ft Lamy)

Lake Chad

Doba

Ngaoundéré

Bouar

Berbérati

CENTRAL AFRICAN REPUBLIC

Bangassou

Bangui

Gemena

Mbandaka (Coquilhatville)

Z A I R E

Kikwit

Kinshasa (Léopoldville)

Brazzaville

C O N G O

Congo

Luobomo

Pte Noire
Cabinda

Tchibanga

G A B O N

Libreville
Port Gentil

EQUATORIAL GUINEA
Bata

Bight of Biafra

Douala
Yaoundé

C A M E R O O N

Dar Rounga

OCEAN

SEYCHELLES

COMOROS

MADAGASCAR (MALAGASY REP.)

MADAGASCAR (MALAGASY REP.)

at the same scale 50

Antananarivo (Tananarive)

Mahajanga (Majunga)

Fianarantsoa

Toamasina (Tamatave)

Antananarivo (Tananarive)

Fianarantsoa

Toliara

Taolanaro

Tropic of Capricorn

at the same scale

MAURITIUS

Mozambique Channel

MADAGASCAR (MALAGASY REP.)

Mtwara

Pemba

Nampula

Quelimane

Sofala (Beira)

Teteo

Inhambane

Mbamba Bay

L. Nyasa

MALAWI

Lilongwe

Blantyre

Chipata

Sumbawanga

Kasama

MOZAMBIQUE

Xai Xai

Mabalane

Mutare

Harare (Salisbury)

Nyanda

ZIMBABWE

Maputo (Lourenço Marques)

SWAZI-LAND

NATAL

Durban

Lubumbashi (Elisabethville)

Mufulira

Ndola

Kamina

Chililabombwe

Luanshya

Likasi (Jadotville)

ZAMBIA

Lusaka

Mazabuka

Zambezi

Kariba Dam

Maramba (Livingstone)

Victoria Falls

Bulawayo

Zambezi

Francistown

Maun

Mongu

Zambezi

BOTSWANA

Kalahari Desert

Mahalapye

Gaborone

Drakensberg

TRANSVAAL

Pretoria

Johannesburg

Welkom

ORANGE FREE STATE

Kimberley

Bloemfontein

LESOTHO

East London

Orange

SOUTH AFRICA

CAPE PROVINCE

ANGOLA

Malange

Luanda

Lobito

Huambo (Nova Lisboa)

Cuchi

Lubango

Capenda Camulemba

Dilu

Tsumeb

NAMIBIA (S.W. AFRICA)

Windhoek

Keetmanshoop

Orange

Walvis Bay (SA)

Namib Desert

ATLANTIC OCEAN

Tropic of Capricorn

Cape Town

Table Mtn 1087▲

Cape of Good Hope

ATLANTIC OCEAN

1:40M

400 800 1200 1600 km
400 800 mis

6 The bullet train and Mount Fuji-san, Japan

7 The Taj Mahal, India

8 Mount Everest, Nepal

ICELAND
ARCTIC OCEAN
Arctic Circle

PORT.
SPAIN
IRELAND
Dublin
London
UNITED KINGDOM
Edinburgh
Netherlands
DENMARK
Copenhagen
Oslo
NORWAY
SWEDEN
FINLAND
Helsinki
Stockholm
Riga
Leningrad
Murmansk
Arkhangel'sk
Vorkuta
Novosibirskiye Ostrova

FRANCE
Paris
Bel.
Lux.
W. GERMANY
SWITZ.
POLAND
Warsaw
CZECHOSLOVAKIA
AUSTRIA HUNGARY
ITALY
Marseille
Corse
Rome
Sardegna
YUGOSLAVIA
Alb.
ROMANIA
Bucharest
BULGARIA
GREECE
Athens
Sicily
Tunis
Istanbul
Ankara
TURKEY
CYPRUS
Adana
Beirut LEB.
SYRIA
Halab
Damascus
ISRAEL
Jerusalem
Amman
JOR.

Moscow
Kiev
Gorkiy
Khar'kov
Odessa
Rostov
Kuybyshev
Astrakhan
Black Sea
Volga
Caspian Sea
Baku
Tbilisi
Sverdlovsk
Chelyabinsk
Omsk
Krasnoyarsk
Novosibirsk
Irkutsk
Yakutsk
Lena
Yenisey
Ob'

UNION OF SOVIET SOCIALIST REPUBLIC

LIBYA
Alexandria
Cairo
EGYPT
Aswân
Nile
SUDAN
Khartoum
RED SEA
SAUDI ARABIA
Mecca
Riyadh
Medina
BAHRAIN
QATAR
Abu Dhabi
U.A.E.
The Gulf
KUWAIT
IRAQ
Baghdad
Basra
Abadan
IRAN
Tehran
Esfahan
Mashhad
Tabriz
Mosul
Kermân
Ashkhabad
Tashkent
Alma Ata
Ürümqi
SINKIANG

MONGOLIA
Ulaanbaatar
INNER MONGOLIA

AFGHANISTAN
Kabul
Herat
Kandahar
Islamabad
Kashmir
PAKISTAN
Lahore
Karachi
Hyderâbâd
Indus
Delhi
Kânpur
Lucknow
NEPAL
Kathmandu
BHUTAN
Thimbu
TIBET
Lhasa
CHINA
Lanzhou
Chengdu
Chongqing
Taiyuan
Zhengzhou
Xi'an
Guiyang
Kunming

Muscat
OMAN
YEMEN
San'a'
S. YEMEN
Aden
G. of Aden
DJIBOUTI
ETHIOPIA
Addis Ababa
Asmara
SOMALIA
Mogadishu
KENYA
Mombasa
Equator
TANZANIA
Dar es Salaam
MOZAMBIQUE
COMOROS
MADAGASCAR
Antananarivo

ARABIAN SEA
Socotra (S Yemen)
Aldabra Is (Sey.)

INDIA
Ahmadâbâd
Bombay
Nâgpur
Jabalpur
Godâvari
Krishna
Hyderabad
Bangalore
Madras
Madurai
SRI LANKA
Colombo
Kandy
Patna
Ganga
Calcutta
BANGLA-DESH
Dhâka
Chittagong
Imphal
Brahmaputra
BURMA
Mandalay
Rangoon
Moulmein
Irrawaddy
Chiang Mai
THAILAND
Bangkok
Vientiane
LAOS
Hanoi
Haiphong
VIETNAM
CAMBODIA (KAMPUCHEA)
Phnom Penh
Ho-Chi-Minh
Surat Thani
George Town
Kuala Lumpur
SINGAPORE
MALAYSIA
SUMATRA
Padang
Palembang
Jakarta

Bay of Bengal
Andaman Is (Ind.)
Nicobar Is (Ind.)
INDIAN OCEAN
Cocos Is (Aust.)

Chang Jiang

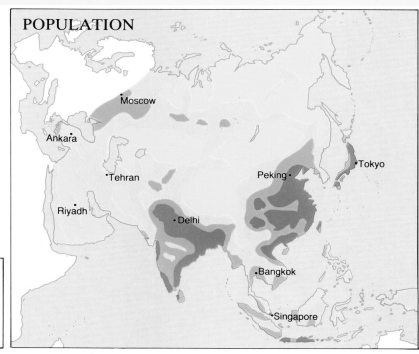

POPULATION

- over 500 persons per km^2
- 100-500 persons per km^2
- 5-100 persons per km^2
- under 5 persons per km^2

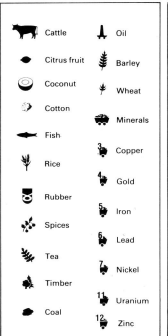

Cattle		Oil	
Citrus fruit		Barley	
Coconut		Wheat	
Cotton		Minerals	
Fish	3	Copper	
Rice	4	Gold	
Rubber	5	Iron	
Spices	6	Lead	
Tea	7	Nickel	
Timber	11	Uranium	
Coal	12	Zinc	

NATURAL VEGETATION/PRODUCTS

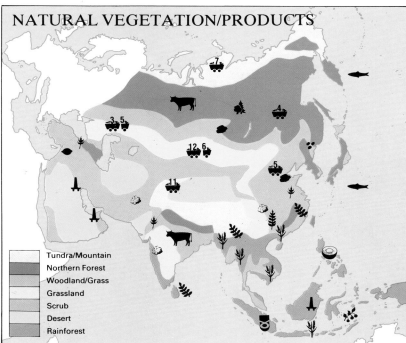

- Tundra/Mountain
- Northern Forest
- Woodland/Grass
- Grassland
- Scrub
- Desert
- Rainforest

DID YOU KNOW THAT …?

1 The world's heaviest bell is the *Czar Bell* in Moscow's Kremlin. It weighs a massive 196 tonnes (193 tons) and is 5.87 m (19 ft 3 in) high! The bell was cast in 1735. It is now cracked, and hasn't been rung since 1836.

2 In Siberia, USSR, there is a huge forest called the *taiga*, which makes up a quarter of the total area of forest in the world! The trees are mostly evergreens – pine and larch. Few people used to live in the taiga, as it is a very cold area, but because it is rich in minerals more people are moving into the forest. They live in industrial towns being built deep in its heart, to exploit the minerals.

3 The huge Gobi Desert covers much of Mongolia. The Gobi is a cold, barren region of rocky plains and hills. Water is very scarce and only a few nomads live here. They exist mainly by cattle raising and live in an unusual tent called a *yurt*, which is shaped like an upside-down bowl.

4 The Great Wall of China stretches for 3460 km (2150 miles), making it the longest in the world. It was built for defence in the 3rd century BC and kept in good repair until 400 years ago. Although part of the wall was blown up to make a dam in 1979, the many remaining sections of the wall are still impressive.

11 Floating vegetable market, Thailand

14 Singapore

12 Bangkok, Thailand

5 Cliff dwellings in Cappadocia, Turkey

13 Water buffalo ploughing Chinese paddy fields

DID YOU KNOW THAT …?

5 In central Turkey, near Urgup in the region called Cappadocia, an extraordinary landscape can be seen. There was once a plateau here, made up of layers of rock, some hard and some much softer. Over thousands of years the softer rocks have been eroded by the weather, by streams and even by men digging out caves to live in. The rocks are now shaped into strange cones, towers and 'mushrooms', with 'hats' of harder rock balancing on top! There are also complete 'villages' of caves connected to each other by passageways cut through the rock. Each cave has 'cupboards' and 'shelves' cut into its walls. Here many centuries ago people hid from religious persecution. Over 300 churches which they dug out of the rock have been found. Some people still live in caves in this region, today.

6 The Seikan Tunnel in Japan is the longest tunnel in the world! It is an underwater tunnel, stretching for 54 km (34 miles). It was built for Japan's famous *bullet train*, the first passenger train to travel at 200 kph.

7 There should have been two Taj Mahals in India – a black one and a white one! In 1648, Emperor Shah Jahan completed the present Taj Mahal. It was a tomb for his wife, and made of white marble. He then began building a tomb of black marble for himself. Before work had got very far, he was overthrown.

8 At 8848 m (29 028 ft) the peak of Mt Everest in the Himalayas is the Earth's highest point! In May 1953, New Zealander Sir Edmund Hillary was the first man to climb Everest. Twenty two years later, in 1975, the first woman to reach the summit was Junko Tabei of Japan.

9 In India cows are sacred animals and are allowed to wander freely, even in the centre of big cities! Drivers are used to going round cows lying peacefully in the middle of the road.

10 Banyan trees can be seen in India and Sri Lanka. They are very unusual to look at, because what seems to be several trees growing close together, is actually just one tree! Aerial roots grow down from the banyan's branches and root in the ground. They become extra 'trunks' and support a huge canopy of leaves, which gives a lot of shade, very useful in such a hot climate.

11 Throughout Asia there are areas where many people live on boats – because there is not enough room for them to live in houses on land (or they cannot afford to) or because they just prefer to live on water. In these places, even the shops are on boats!

4 The Great Wall, China

0 Banyan tree, India

9 Street in India

2 Bangkok, Thailand, once had many canals, called *klongs*, instead of roads. (The city was called the 'Venice of the East' because the klongs reminded visitors of the canals in Venice, Italy.) They were used for transport and also helped to drain the land during the rainy season. After cars and lorries began to be used for transport, many of the klongs were filled in to make roads. Now Bangkok has problems with flooding when the monsoons come.

3 Paddy fields, the irrigated fields in which rice is grown, get their name from *padi*, the Malayan word for rice. Rice is grown throughout Asia in the fertile lowlands near the equator. Millions of people live in these areas, and rice is very important to them as it yields more food per acre than any other crop.

4 Over half the population of the world lives in Asia – that is 2 782 000 000 people! Some parts of Asia have many people living in a small area. One of the most densely populated countries is Singapore, which has an average of 4 039 people for each square kilometre of ground!

AFGHANISTAN

Area: 674 500 sq km
(260 424 sq miles)
Population: 14 400 000
Capital: Kabul
Languages: Pashtu, Dari, Uzbek
Currency: Afghani

INDONESIA

Area: 1 919 263 sq km
(741 027 miles)
Population: 161 600 000
Capital: Jakarta
Language: Bahasa
(Indonesian)
Currency: Rupiah

ISRAEL

Area: 20 770 sq km
(8019 sq miles)
Population: 4 200 000
Capital: Jerusalem
Languages: Hebrew, Arabic
Currency: Shekel

PAKISTAN

Area: 803 941 sq km
(310 402 sq miles)
Population: 97 300 000
Capital: Islamabad
Language: Urdu
Currency: Pakistan Rupee

THAILAND

Area: 513 517 sq km
(198 269 sq miles)
Population: 51 700 000
Capital: Bangkok
Languages: Thai, Chinese
Currency: Baht

CHINA

Area: 9 561 000 sq km
(3 691 502 sq miles)
Population: 1'034 500 000
Capital: Peking
Language: Chinese
(Mandarin)
Currency: Yuan

IRAN

Area: 1 648 184 sq km
(636 364 sq miles)
Population: 43 800 000
Capital: Tehran
Language: Persian (Farsi)
Currency: Rial

JAPAN

Area: 371 000 sq km
(143 243 sq miles)
Population: 119 900 000
Capital: Tokyo
Language: Japanese
Currency: Yen

SAUDI ARABIA

Area: 2 400 930 sq km
(927 000 sq miles)
Population: 10 800 000
Capital: Riyadh
Language: Arabic
Currency: Riyal

TURKEY

Area: 780 576 sq km
(301 380 sq miles)
Population: 50 200 000
Capital: Ankara
Language: Turkish
Currency: Turkish Lira

INDIA

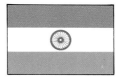

Area: 3 287 593 sq km
(1 269 340 sq miles)
Population: 746 400 000
Capital: Delhi
Languages: Hindi, English
Currency: Indian Rupee

IRAQ

Area: 434 924 sq km
(167 924 sq miles)
Population: 15 000 000
Capital: Baghdad
Language: Arabic
Currency: Iraqi Dinar

MALAYSIA

Area: 330 669 sq km
(127 671 sq miles)
Population: 15 300 000
Capital: Kuala Lumpur
Language: Malay
Currency: Ringgit
(Malaysian Dollar)

SINGAPORE

Area: 616 sq km
(238 sq miles)
Population: 2 500 000
Capital: Singapore
Languages: Chinese, Malay, Tamil, English
Currency: Singapore Dollar

USSR

Area: 22 402 000 sq km
(8 649 412 sq miles)
Population: 274 000 000
Capital: Moscow
Language: Russian
Currency: Ruble

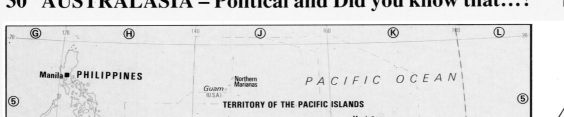

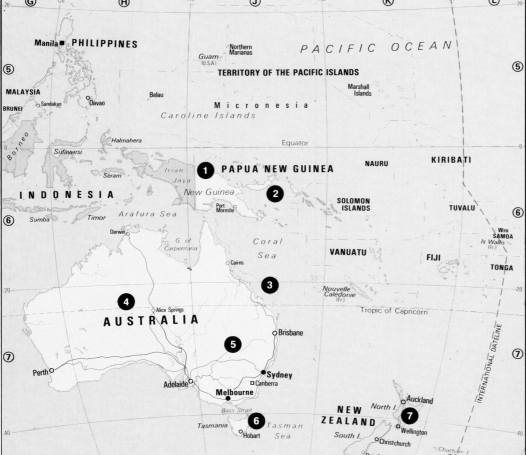

7 Geysers at Whakarewarewa, New Zealand

DID YOU KNOW THAT ...?

1 Over 700 languages are spoken in Papua New Guinea! That is more than a quarter of all the languages spoken in the world! Papua New Guinea's mountains, thick forests and islands meant that different tribes did not mix, so they did not share a common language, but instead each developed its own. Today, Pidgin English and Police Motu have become the languages which the different tribes use to talk to each other.

2 No less than 38 different species of the beautiful Bird of Paradise are to be seen in Papua New Guinea! Another 5 species are found on neighbouring islands and in northern Australia. Their tail feathers are a traditional part of Papua New Guinea tribal costume, although the birds are now protected from hunting to a great extent.

3 Australia's Great Barrier Reef is formed from the shells of millions of tiny sea creatures! It is 2000 km (1250 miles) long and is the world's biggest coral reef. There are many thousands of coral islands or *atolls* in the Pacific region.

4 Ayers Rock is a huge sandstone rock formation which rears up abruptly from the desert in central Australia. The rock is special because it changes colour with the light. Australia's native *aborigine* people believe there is something magical about the rock.

5 Australia is the driest of all the continents in the world! Rainfall is also very unevenly distributed: even though the tropical north has about 2000 mm (79 inches) a year, the central deserts have less than 150 mm (6 inches). Irrigation is important for agriculture, and rivers and artesian wells are used as a source of water. The Snowy Mountains reservoir and irrigation scheme has brought water from the mountains to irrigate farmland in the east of Australia.

6 A Tasmanian Devil is a little bear-like creature found only in Tasmania. It is just 60 cm (2 feet) long, with a big bushy tail. It has very sharp teeth and eats other

4 Ayers Rock, Australia

6 Tasmanian Devil

POPULATION

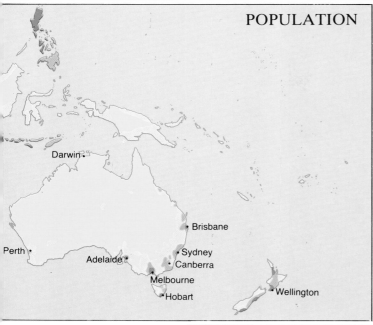

NATURAL VEGETATION/PRODUCTS

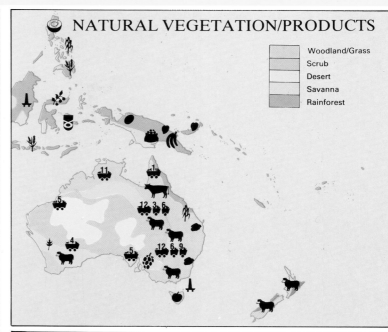

Woodland/Grass
Scrub
Desert
Savanna
Rainforest

Population key

	over 500 persons per km²
	100-500 persons per km²
	5-100 persons per km²
	under 5 persons per km²

Products key

Sheep	Coffee	Coal	Minerals
Apples	Cocoa	Oil	1 Bauxite
Bananas	Rubber	Spices	3 Copper
Grapes	Yams	Sugar cane	4 Gold
Coconut	Rice	Wheat	5 Iron

6	Lead
9	Silver
11	Uranium
12	Zinc

2 Traditional dress, Papua New Guinea

nimals and small birds when it comes out at night. The Tasmanian evil is a *marsupial*. This means it arries its young in a pouch.

The tallest geyser ever to have erupted was the Waimangu eyser in New Zealand. In 1904 it ose to a height of 457 m (1500 ft). last erupted in 1917, killing four eople! Today, steam from New ealand's hot springs and geysers is arnessed to generate electricity.

3 The Great Barrier Reef, Australia

AUSTRALIA

Area: 7 682 300 sq km (2 966 136 sq miles)
Population: 15 500 000
Capital: Canberra
Language: English
Currency: Australian Dollar

NEW ZEALAND

Area: 268 675 sq km (103 735 sq miles)
Population: 3 200 000
Capital: Wellington
Language: English
Currency: New Zealand Dollar

TONGA

Area: 699 sq km (270 sq miles)
Population: 97 000
Capital: Nuku'alofa
Languages: English, Tongan
Currency: Pa'anga

FIJI

Area: 18 272 sq km (7055 sq miles)
Population: 700 000
Capital: Suva
Languages: English, Fijian
Currency: Fiji Dollar

PAPUA NEW GUINEA

Area: 461 692 sq km (178 259 sq miles)
Population: 3 400 000
Capital: Port Moresby
Languages: English, Melanesian Pidgin
Currency: Kina

VANUATU

Area: 14 763 sq km (5700 sq miles)
Population: 100 000
Capital: Vila
Languages: Bislama, English, French
Currency: Australian Dollar, Vatu

KIRIBATI

Area: 800 sq km (309 sq miles)
Population: 59 000
Capital: Tarawa
Languages: English, I Kiribati
Currency: Australian Dollar

SOLOMON ISLANDS

Area: 29 785 sq km (11 500 sq miles)
Population: 300 000
Capital: Honiara
Languages: English, Pidgin
Currency: Solomon Islands Dollar

WESTERN SAMOA

Area: 2831 sq km (1093 sq miles)
Population: 200 000
Capital: Apia
Languages: Samoan, English
Currency: Tala

1:20M

200 400 600 800 km
200 400 mls

Glasgow
U.K.
SCOTLAND

Arctic Circle

NORWEGIAN SEA

② ③ ② B C D E F G H

ARCTI

SPITSBERGEN (Nor.)

FRANZ-JOSEF-LAND

BARENTS SEA

NOVAYA ZEMLYA

KARA SEA

North Sea
DENMARK
Copenhagen (København)
Hamburg
GERMANY
W   E
Berlin
POLAND
Poznań Łódź
Wrocław Kraków
L'vov
Carpathian Mts

BALTIC SEA

Stockholm

SWEDEN

NORWAY

Lappland
Nordkapp

Murmansk
Kol'skiy Poluostrov
White Sea (Beloye More)

FINLAND
Helsinki
Novgorod
Leningrad
Petrozavodsk
Karel'skaya A.S.S.R.
Arkhangel'sk
Vorkuta

Gydanskiy Poluostrov

ESTONSKAYA S.S.R.
Riga
LATVIYSKAYA S.S.R.
LITOVSKAYA S.S.R.

BELO-RUSSKAYA S.S.R.
Minsk

MOLDAVSKAYA S.S.R.

UKRAINSKAYA S.S.R.
Kiyev
Krivoy Rog
Dnepropetrovsk
Zaporozh'ye
Donetsk
Khar'kov
Odessa
Sevastopol'

BLACK SEA

Dnepr
Smolensk
Bryansk
Tula
Moscow (Moskva)
Yaroslavl'
Koloma
Voronezh
Vologda
Kirov
Syktyvkar
Komi R.A.S.S.R.
Olzhevsk
Perm'
Udmurtskaya A.S.S.R.

Gor'kiy
Mariyskaya S.S.R.
Mordovskaya A.S.S.R.
Kazan
Tatarskaya A.S.S.R.
Saratov
Kuybyshev
Ufa
Bashkirskaya A.S.S.R.
Magnitogorsk

Sverdlovsk
Chelyabinsk

ROSSIYS

Zapadno Sibirskaya Nizmennost

Tomsk
Omsk
Novosibirsk
Novokuznetsk
Barnaul
Ob'

Rostov-na-Donu
Volgograd
Krasnodar
Novorossiysk
Maykop
Kalmytskaya A.S.S.R.
Astrakhan'
Ural'sk
Volga
Aktyubinsk

CASPIAN SEA

Kokchetav
Karaganda
Semipalatinsk

TURKEY
Yerevan
Tbilisi
GRUZINSKAYA S.S.R.
ARMYANSKAYA S.S.R.
AZERBAYDZHANSKAYA S.S.R.
Baku
Tabriz
Tehrān
IRAQ
IRAN

Dagestanskaya A.S.S.R.

KAZAKHSKAYA S.S.R.

Aral'skoye More
Kara-Kalpakskaya A.S.S.R.
Kzyl Orda
Ozero Balkhash

TURKMENSKAYA S.S.R.
UZBEKSKAYA S.S.R.
Tashkent
Leninabad
Karshi
Alma Ata
Urümqi
KIRGIZSKAYA S.S.R.
Tien Shan
Pik Pobedy 7439

TADZHIKSKAYA S.S.R.
Pik Kommunizma 7495
Pamir

AFGHANISTAN

SINKIA

② Bering Str.

③

70

⑪ ⑫ ⑬ ⑭ ⑮ 60

170

100 110 120 130 140 150 160 170 80 70

⑫ M ⑬ N ⑭ O ⑮ P ⑯ Q ⑰ R ⑱ S ⑲ T ② ⑳ U

L M N O A

O C E A N

NORTH LAND

LAPTEV
SEA

NEW SIBERIAN ISLANDS

EAST SIBERIAN
SEA

Kolymskaya
Nizmennost'

Kolymskoye Nagor'ye

Koryakskoye Nagor'ye

BERING
SEA

180

T
④

luostrov
Taymyr

Khrebet Cherskogo

K A M C H A T K A

Petropavlovsk-
Kamchatskiy

Magadan

sk

Yakutskay

A.Verkhoyanskiy Khrebet

S. S. R.

SEA
OF
OKHOTSK

S

R
⑤

Yakutsk

Lena

Kuril'skiye Ostrova
(Kuril Islands)

SAKHALIN

Y A S. F. S. R.

Sredne

Lena

Stanovoy Khrebet

Komsomol'sk
na-Amure

Amur

Tatarskiy Proliv

Yuzhno-Sakhalinsk

Sibirskoye

Ploskogor'ye

Yenisey

Bratst

Baykal

Buryatskaya
A.S.S.R.

Blagoveshchensk

Xiao Hinggan Ling

Khabarovsk

Sikhote Alin'

HOKKAIDO
Sapporo

Q

oyarsk
Yenise

Cheremkhovo

Irkutsk

Ulan Ude

Chita

Oze

De Hinggan Ling

Qiqihar

M A N C H U R I A

Ussuriysk Nakhodka

Vladivostok

Sendai

uvinskaya A.S.S.R.

Manzhouli

Harbin

SEA
OF

Sühbaatar

Choybalsan

Changchun Jilin

JAPAN

140

JAPAN

Ulaanbaatar

Fushun

NORTH
KOREA

H O N S H U

Tōkyō
⑥

M O N G O L I A

G O B I

Shenyang

Benxi

Yokohama

Nagoya

A I

INNER MONGOLIA

Jinzhou Anshan

P'yŏngyang

Seoul
(Sŏul)

SOUTH
KOREA

Kyōto Kōbe Osaka

Lüda

Ch'ŏngju

Taegu

Hiroshima

Hohhot

Tangshan

Inch'ŏn

Pusan

Kita-
Kyūshū Shikoku

N

Baotou

Peking
(Beijing)

Fukuoka

Tientsin
(Tianjin)

Kwangju

G C H

Taiyuan

Shijiazhuang

Qingdao

YELLOW

130

L

Yinchuan

M

GREAT
WALL

Handan

Jinan

SEA

N

Xuzhou

O

110 120

100

1:20M

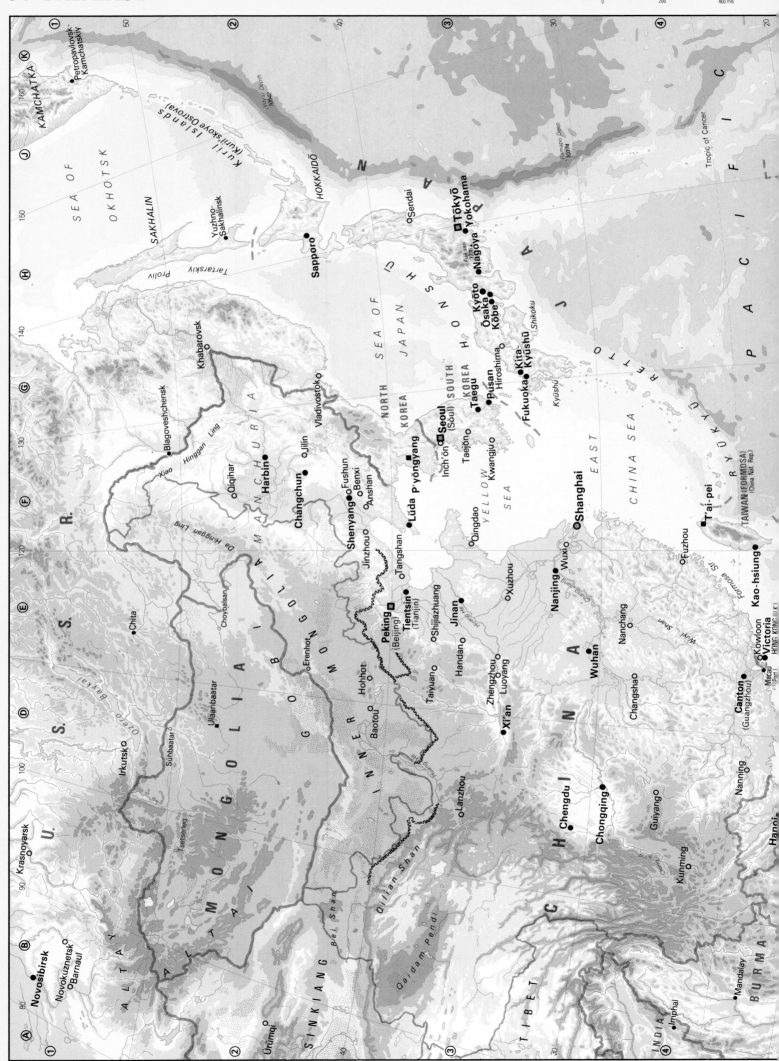

200   400   600   800 km
200   400 mls

Ⓚ KAMCHATKA

Petropavlovsk-Kamchatskiy

SEA OF OKHOTSK

Kuril'skoye Ostrova)
Kurili Islands

SAKHALIN

Proliv Tatarskiy

Yuzhno-Sakhalinsk

HOKKAIDŌ

Sapporo

Vpdna Deep 10542

Khabarovsk

Blagoveshchensk

Xiao Hinggan Ling

MANCHURIA

Qiqihar

Harbin

Jilin

Vladivostok

Changchun

Fushun

Shenyang

Benxi

Anshan

Jinzhou

Da Hinggan Ling

R.

U.

S.

S.

Chita

Choybalsan

Erenhot

MONGOLIA

Ulaanbaatar

Sühbaatar

Irkutsk

ozero Baykal

Tsetserleg

Krasnoyarsk

Novosibirsk

Novokuznetsk

Barnaul

ALTAY

SINKIANG

Ürümqi

Hohhot

Baotou

INNER MONGOLIA

Lanzhou

Bei Shan

Qilian Shan

Qaidam Pendi

TIBET

Kunming

Nanning

BURMA

Mandalay

Imphal

INDIA

Hanoi

NORTH KOREA

SEA OF JAPAN

HONSHŪ

Sendai

Tōkyō

Yokohama

Nagoya

Fuji-san 3776

Kyōto

Ōsaka

Kōbe

Hiroshima

Kita-Kyūshū

Fukuoka

Shikoku

Kyūshū

SOUTH KOREA

Seoul (Sŏul)

Inch'ŏn

P'yŏngyang

Taejŏn

Taegu

Pusan

Kwangju

YELLOW SEA

Lüda

Tangshan

Jinan

Peking (Beijing)

Tientsin (Tianjin)

Shijiazhuang

Taiyuan

Handan

Zhengzhou

Luoyang

Xi'an

Huang He

Huang He

CHINA

Nanjing

Wuxi

Xuzhou

Shanghai

EAST CHINA SEA

Fuzhou

Chang Jiang

Nanchang

Wuhan

Changsha

Chengdu

Chongqing

Guiyang

Qingdao

RYŪKYŪ RETTŌ

Tropic of Cancer

Ramapo Deep 10374

PACIFIC

TAIWAN (FORMOSA) (China Nat. Rep.)

T'ai-pei

Kao-hsiung

Formosa Str.

Wuyi Shan

Kowloon

Victoria

HONG KONG (U.K.)

Macau (Port.)

Canton (Guangzhou)

⑦

⑧

Ⓗ

Port
Moresby ■

C O R A L   S E A

PAPUA

NEW GUINEA

Great   Barrier   Reef

Equator

IRIAN

JAYA

Cape
York

Ⓗ

140

Trust Terr. of the PACIFIC ISLANDS (USA)

C A R O L I N E   I S L A N D S

O   C   E   A   N

Ⓖ

Gulf   of

Carpentaria

○Darwin

AUSTRALIA

Ⓖ

130

MINDANAO

MOLUCCAS

CERAM SEA

B A N D A   S E A

ARAFURA   SEA

A R A F U R A   S E A

LUZON

PHILIPPINES

Quezon City

Manila ■

General
Santos ●

Manado ●

CELEBES
SEA

CELEBES
(SULAWESI)

TIMOR

T I M O R   S E A

Ⓕ

120

Ⓕ

SOUTH

S U L U

S E A

Makassar
(Ujung Pandang) ●

I N D O N E S I A

Ⓔ

Banjarmasin ●

Surabaya ●

Ⓔ

110

CHINA

B R U N E I

SARAWAK

BORNEO

KALIMANTAN

J A V A   S E A

Mouths of
the Mekong

INDO-

CHINA

SEA

MALAYSIA

Pontianak ●

Semarang ○

J A V A

I N D I A N

Vientiane ■

Mekong

Saigon (Ho Chi Minh) ●

Jakarta □

Bandung ●

O C E A N

THAILAND

CAMBODIA
(KAMPUCHEA)

VIETNAM

Phnom Penh ■

Kuala Lumpur ■

SINGAPORE

Palembang ○

S U M A T R A

Ⓓ

Bangkok ■

Rangoon ■

Mouths of
the Irrawaddy

ANDAMAN
SEA

○Medan

Ⓒ

⑤

⑥

⑦

⑧

MONGOLIA

G O B I

I N N E R

M O N G O L I A

Yin Shan

Hohhot ○
Baotou ○

Peking ■
(Beijing)

○ Tangshan

H e b e i

Tientsin
(Tianjin) ●

BO HAI

Dairen ●
(Lüda)

Shenyang ●
L i a o n i n g
Jinzhou ○   Anshan ○

Ningxia

Taiyuan ○

S h a n x i

○ Shijiazhuang

○ Handan

Tsinan
(Jinan) ●
S h a n d o n g

○ Tsingtao
(Qingdao)

YELLOW SE

Qinghai
Lanzhou ○
Huang He

Huang He

S h a a n x i

Sian ●
(Xi'an)

Qin Ling

Luoyang ○
○ Zhengzhou

H e n a n

Huang He

○ Xuzhou

J i a n g s u

C   H   I   N   A

Daba Shan

Nanking ●
(Nanjing)

A n h u i
Dabie Shan

Wuxi
Suzhou ○
Tai Hu

Shang

H u b e i

Wuhan ●

Chang Jiang

Chang Jiang

Hangzhou ○

Chengdu ●

S i c h u a n

Chang Jiang

Z h e j i a n g

Daxue Shan

Chungking ●
(Chongqing)

Wuling Shan

Mufu Shan

Poyang
Hu
○ Nanchang

Dalou Shan

○ Changsha

H u n a n

J i a n g x i

G u i z h o u
○ Guiyang

Luoxiao Shan

F u j i a n
○ Foochow
(Fuzhou)

FORMOSA   STRAIT

T'ai-

○ Kunming

Y u n n a n

Nan   Ling

TAIWA

G u a n g x i

G u a n g d o n g

Kao-hsiung ●

○ Nanning

Canton ●
(Guangzhou)

○ Kowloon
Victoria
Macau ○
(Port)   HONG KONG (U.K.)

V I E T N A M

S O U T H

■ **Hanoi**

L A O S

C H I N A

S E A

HAINAN DAO

1:10M

	100	200	300	400 km
0				
0	100		200 mls	

SEA OF OKHOTSK

○ Okha

U. S. S. R.

SAKHALIN

INNER
MONGOLIA

Blagoveshchensk ●

Komsomol'sk-
na-Amure ●

50

Uglegorsk ○

Xiao Hinggan Ling

Hinggan Ling

○ Qiqihar

Heilongjiang

CHINA

Khabarovsk ●

Yuzhno-Sakhalinsk ●

②

MANCHURIA

● Harbin

Tatarskiy Proliv

45

Mudanjiang ●

Asahikawa ●

Changchun ●   ● Jilin

Jilin

Ussuriysk ●

Vladivostok ○

Sapporo ●

Kushiro ●

③

● Liaoyuan

Nakhodka ●

HOKKAIDŌ

Khrebet Sikhote Alin'

● Muroran

iaoning   ○ Fushun
Shenyang ●
○ Benxi
nshan

Changbai ○   ● Ch'ŏngjin

Hakodate ●

Kanggye ●

Hamgyong Sanmaek

● Kimch'aek

Aomori ●

N

**NORTH
KOREA**

SEA OF

40

Hüngnam ●

JAPAN

Akita ●   Morioka ●

Nangnim Sanmaek

P'yŏngyang ■   ● Wŏnsan

○ Namp'o

Sendai ○

④

Haeju ●

Taebaek Sanmaek

Inch'ŏn ○ ■**Seoul**
(Sŏul)

HONSHŪ

Nagaoka ●
Mikuni-sammyaku

A

YELLOW SEA

Taejŏn ○

**SOUTH
KOREA**

Kanazawa ●
Matsumoto ●

Hitachi ●

PACIFIC

Taegu ●

Matsue ●

Tōkyō ■
Kawasaki ■   ○ Chiba
Fuji-san ▲ 3776   ■**Yokohama**

OCEAN

Kwangju ○

Pusan ●

Okayama ○

**Kyōto ●
Kōbe** ●

Nagoya ●

35

Yŏsu ●

Hiroshima ○

Osaka ●
○ Sakai

Shizuoka ●

P

Kita-Kyūshū ●
Fukuoka ●

Matsuyama ●

Korea Strait

Takamatsu ●

A

Nagasaki ●

SHIKOKU

J

● Kumamoto

KYŪSHŪ

⑤

Kagoshima ●

30

125   B   130   C   135   D   140   E   145   F

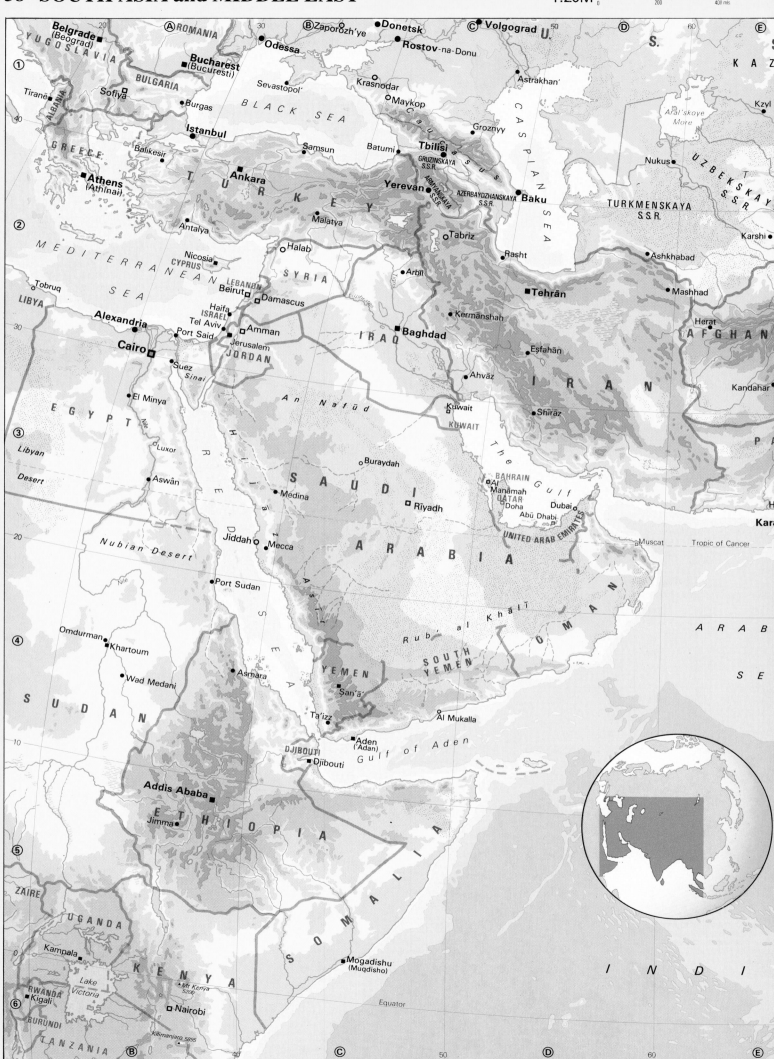

38 SOUTH ASIA and MIDDLE EAST

Scale 1:20M

| 0 | 200 | 400 | 600 | 800 km |
| 0 | 200 | 400 mls |

Belgrade (Beograd)
YUGOSLAVIA
ROMANIA
Bucharest (Bucuresti)
Zaporozh'ye
Donetsk
Volgograd
U.S.S.R.
Odessa
Rostov-na-Donu
KAZ
Tiranë
ALBANIA
BULGARIA
Sofiya
Burgas
Sevastopol'
Krasnodar
Astrakhan'
Aral'skoye More
Kzyl
Istanbul
BLACK SEA
Maykop
CASPIAN SEA
Nukus
UZBEKSKAYA S.S.R.
GREECE
Balıkesir
Samsun
Batumi
Groznyy
Tbilisi
Athens (Athínai)
Ankara
T U R K E Y
GRUZINSKAYA S.S.R.
ARMYANSKAYA S.S.R.
AZERBAYDZHANSKAYA S.S.R.
Baku
TURKMENSKAYA S.S.R.
Ashkhabad
Karshi
Antalya
Malatya
Yerevan
Tabriz
Rasht
Halab
SYRIA
Arbil
MEDITERRANEAN SEA
Nicosia
CYPRUS
LEBANON
Beirut
Damascus
Tehrân
Mashhad
Tobruq
Haifa
ISRAEL
Tel Aviv
Amman
Kermānshah
Esfahān
Herat
AFGHAN
Alexandria
Port Said
Jerusalem
JORDAN
IRAQ
Baghdad
I R A N
LIBYA
Cairo
Suez
Sinai
Ahvāz
Kandahar
El Minya
An Nafūd
Kuwait
Shīrāz
PA
EGYPT
KUWAIT
Libyan
Nile
Buraydah
BAHRAIN
Al Manāmah
QATAR
Doha
Dubai
Kar
Desert
Aswân
S A U D I
Medina
Rīyadh
Abū Dhabi
UNITED ARAB EMIRATES
Muscat
Tropic of Cancer
Jiddah
Mecca
A R A B I A
The Gulf
Nubian Desert
Nile
O M A N
A R A B
Port Sudan
Rub' al Khālī
S E
RED SEA
SOUTH YEMEN
Omdurman
Khartoum
Asmara
YEMEN
San'ā'
Al Mukalla
SUDAN
Wad Medani
Ta'izz
Aden (Adan)
Gulf of Aden
DJIBOUTI
Djibouti
Addis Ababa
SOMALIA
ZAIRE
UGANDA
ETHIOPIA
Jimma
Kampala
Lake Victoria
KENYA
Mt Kenya 5200
RWANDA
Kigali
BURUNDI
TANZANIA
Kilimanjaro 5895
Nairobi
Mogadishu (Muqdisho)
Equator
INDI

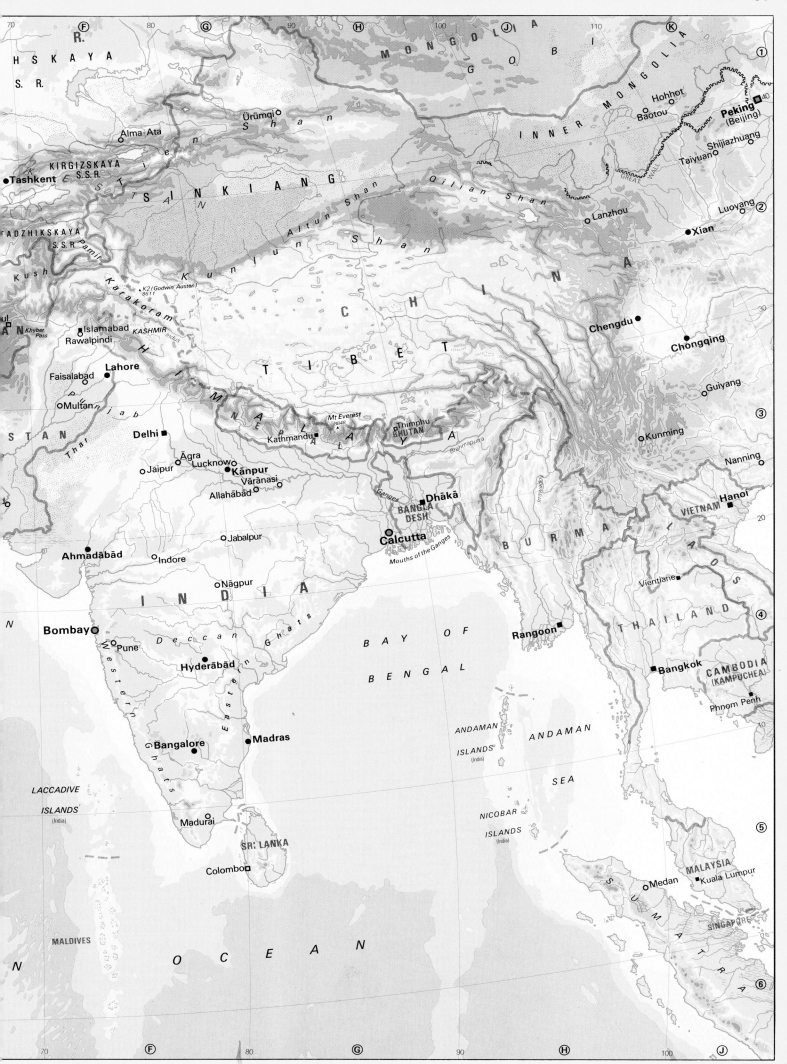

1:10M

Ⓐ 95   Ⓑ 100   Ⓒ 105   Ⓓ   110 Ⓔ

① Nanning
CHINA
Maomi
Pingxiang
Lao Cai
B U R M A
Mandalay
Myingyan
Meiktila
Zhanjiang
Taung-gyi
Hanoi
Haiphong
Gulf of
Pyinmana
Tongkin
Luang
Prabang
Mekong
Haikou
HAINAN
Ya Xian
Chiang Mai
Vinh
INDO
Prome
Muang
Phrae
Vientiane
Udon
Thani
Henzada
Pegu
M.Phitsanulok
Hue
CHINA
Bassein Rangoon
Da Nang
Moulmein
T H A I L A N D
Ubon
Ratchathani
Pakse
Nakhon
Ratchasima
Tavoy
Khong
Qui Nhon
Thon Bangkok
Buri
Sisophon
C A M B O D I A
(K A M P U C H E A)
Ban Me
Thuot
B.Hua
Hin
Da Lat
Nha Trang
Cam Ranh
Kompong
Cham
A N D A M A N
Phnom
Penh
S E A
Mergui
Archipelago
GULF
OF
Chau
Phu
Saigon (Ho Chi Minh)
My Tho
Vung Tau
THAILAND
Rach Gia Can
Tho
Mouths of
the Mekong
Surat
Thani
NICOBAR
ISLANDS
(India)
S O U T H
C H I N A
Ban
Hat Yai
Kota Bharu
S E A
George
Town
Banda Aceh
Kuala Trengganu
M A L A Y S I A
Ipoh
M A L A Y A
Medan
PENINSULAR
MALAYSIA
Pematangsiantar
Kelang
Kuala
Lumpur
SARAWAK
(Malaysia)
Si
Melaka
Kuching
Padangsidempuan
Johor
Bharu
SINGAPORE
Singkawang
B O R N E O
Pekanbaru
Pontianak
Rengat
P.P.Batu
Padang
I N D O N E S I A
Siberut
Jambi

1:7.5M

0 100 200 300 km
0 50 100 150 mls

① ② ③ ④

Baku ●
50
40

Ardabil ○

U. S. S. R.

○ Tabriz

I R A N

Hamadān ●
Kermānshāh ●
Khorramābad ●

Urumiyeh ○

Kirovakan ●
Yerevan ●

K u r d i s t a n

Ahvāz ●
Abādān ●

KUWAIT
Kuwait ●

E

Batumi ●

Erzurum ●

Arbil ●

Kirkūk ●

■ **Baghdād**

An Najaf ●

Basra ●

Hafar al Bātin ○

45

D

B l a c k   S e a

Mosul ●

Tigris

Al Hadithah ○

I R A Q

An Nāsiriyah ○

T U R K E Y

Sivas ●

Malatya ●

Urfa ●

A l   J a z ī r a h

Euphrates

Al Bū Kamāl ○

Ar Rutbah ○

B a d i y a t   a s h   S h ā m

Al Jālamīd ○

A l   W i d i y ā n

○ Sakākah

S A U D I   A R A B I A

40

C

Kuzey Anadolu Dağları

Samsun ●

'Aleppo ●
(Halab)

S Y R I A

Hamāh ●
Hims ●

Damascus ■
(Dimashq)

Amman ●

Jerusalem ■

J O R D A N

At Tisawiyah ○

Al Mudawwara ○

Tabūk ○

Adana ●

Ürgüp ○

Toros Dağları

Al Lādhiqīyah ●

Tripoli ●

Beirut □
(Beyrouth)

LEBANON

Haifa ●
ISRAEL
Tel Aviv Yafo ●
Nazareth ○

Gaza ●

Dead Sea

Beersheba ●

Negev

35

B

■ **Ankara**

Antalya ●

Nicosia ■

CYPRUS

M e d i t e r r a n e a n   S e a

Port Said ●
(Būr Sa'īd)

Suez ●
(El Suweis)

G u l f   o f   S u e z

SINAI

İstanbul ●

Balıkesir ●

İzmir ○

GREECE

Alexandria ●
(El Iskandarīya)

Tanta ●

El Gīza ○ □ **Cairo**
(El Qâ'hira)

E G Y P T

El Minya ●

Qattâra Depression

30

A

① ② ③ ④
40 35 30

1:20M

200 400 600 800 km
200 400 mls

120   130   140   150

Manado
Halmahera
BORNEO
MOLUCCAS
Balikpapan
CELEBES
(SULAWESI)
INDONESIA
Banda Sea
Timor
IRIAN JAYA
Pegunungan Maoke
NEW GUINEA
Bismarck Archipelago
PAPUA
NEW GUINEA
New
New
Port Moresby

①

Arafura Sea
Torres Strait
Great

Timor Sea
Darwin
Gulf of Carpentaria
Barrier

10

INDIAN
OCEAN

②

NORTHERN
TERRITORY
Cairns
Townsville
Islan
Great
Mackay

Dampier
Great Sandy Desert
Alice Springs
Ayers Rock
QUEENSLAND
Dividing

20

WESTERN
AUSTRALIA
AUSTRALIA
Lake Eyre Basin
L. Eyre
SOUTH
AUSTRALIA
Darling

③

Great Victoria Desert
NEW SOUTH
WALES
New
Geraldton
Kalgoorlie
Sydne
Wollongong

Perth
Fremantle
Great Australian Bight
Adelaide
Murray
Canbe
Murray
VICTORIA
Geelong
Melbourne

30

④

Bass Strait
Hobart
TASMAN

40

⑤

110   A   120   B   130   C   140   D   150

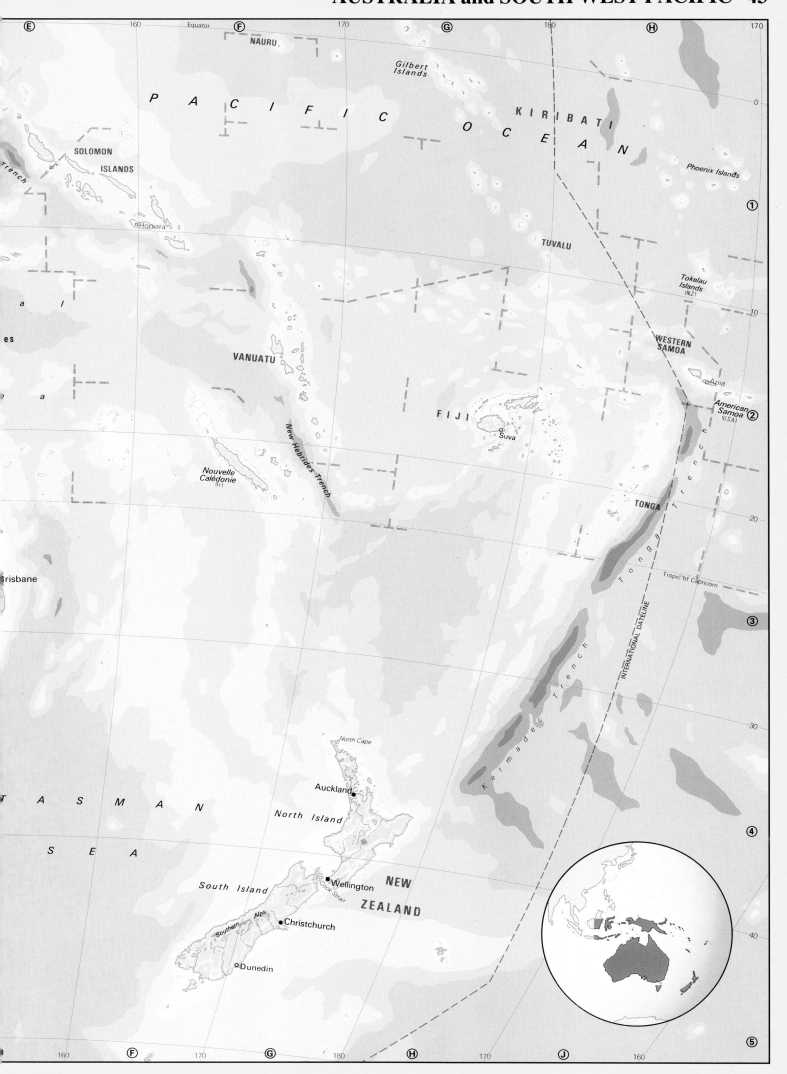

NAURU

Gilbert
Islands

P A C I F I C   O C E A N

K I R I B A T I

Phoenix Islands

SOLOMON

ISLANDS

Trench

□ Honiara

TUVALU

Tokelau
Islands
(N.Z.)

WESTERN
SAMOA

□ Apia

VANUATU

FIJI

American
Samoa
(U.S.A.)

New Hebrides Trench

Suva

Nouvelle
Calédonie
(Fr.)

TONGA

Tropic of Capricorn

Brisbane

Tonga Trench

INTERNATIONAL DATELINE

Kermadec Trench

North Cape

T A S M A N

Auckland

North Island

S E A

South Island

Wellington

Cook Strait

NEW

ZEALAND

Southern

Alps

Christchurch

○ Dunedin

Equator

160 · F · 170 · G · 180 · H · 170

0

①

10

②

20

③

30

④

40

⑤

160 · F · 170 · G · 180 · H · 170 · J · 160

1:5M

0   50   100   150   200 km
0   50   100 mls

Ⓐ   170   Ⓑ

35

TASMAN   SEA

①

Ⓐ   Ⓑ

North Cape

Kaikohe

Whangarei

NORTH ISLAND

Auckland
Manukau

Coromandel Peninsula

Tauranga
Hamilton
Whakatane
Bay of Plenty

Hick Bay

Raukumara Ra.

Huiarau Ra.

L. Taupo
Taupo

Gisborne

New Plymouth

Mt Ruapehu
2797

Hawke Bay

Mahia Peninsu

S. Taranaki Bight

Napier

Wanganui

Ruahine Ra.

Ruatine Ra.

Palmerston N

Masterton

40

C. Farewell

Golden Bay

Tasman Bay

COOK STRAIT

Karamea Bight

Nelson

Wellington

SOUTH ISLAND

Spenser Mts

Kaikoura Ra.

Greymouth

②

SOUTHERN ALPS

Pegasus Bay

Mt Cook
3764

Christchurch

Canterbury Plains

Cascade Pt

Canterbury Bight

Hawkdun Ra.

Timaru

PACIFIC

Cromwell

Oamaru

45

Fiordland
Nat. Park

L. Te Anau

OCEAN

Manapouri

Dunedin

③

Foveaux Strait

Invercargill

Stewart Island

Ⓐ   170   Ⓑ   175   Ⓒ

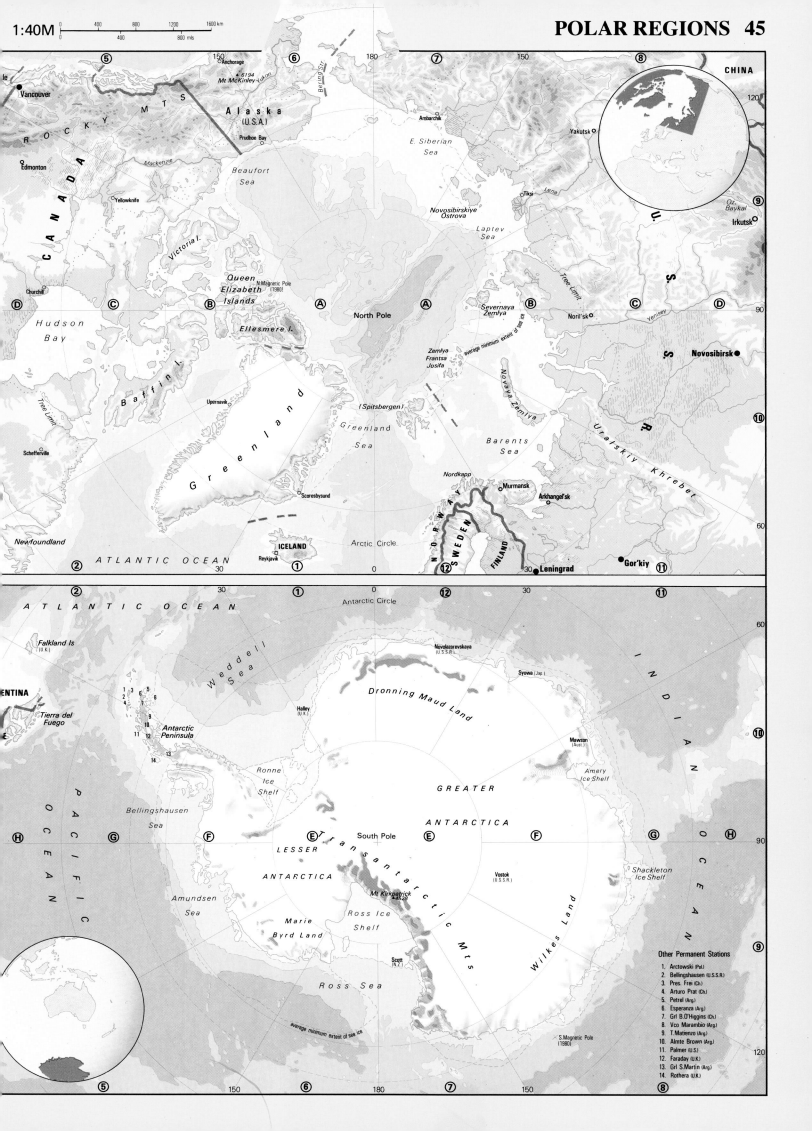

1:40M

400 800 1200 1600 km
400 800 mls

North Polar Region

Vancouver
Anchorage
Mt McKinley ▲ 6194
Yukon
Alaska (U.S.A.)
Prudhoe Bay
Edmonton
Mackenzie
Yellowknife
ROCKY MTS
CANADA
Beaufort Sea
E. Siberian Sea
Ambarchik
Yakutsk
CHINA
Lena
Tiksi
Novosibirskiye Ostrova
Laptev Sea
Tree Limit
Oz. Baykal
Irkutsk
Churchill
Queen Elizabeth Islands
N. Magnetic Pole (1980)
North Pole
Severnaya Zemlya
Noril'sk
Yenisey
U. S. S. R.
Novosibirsk
Hudson Bay
Victoria I.
Ellesmere I.
Baffin I.
average minimum extent of sea ice
Zemlya Frantsa Josifa
Novaya Zemlya
Uralskiy Khrebet
Tree Limit
Upernavik
Greenland
(Spitsbergen)
Greenland Sea
Barents Sea
Schefferville
Scoresbysund
Nordkapp
Murmansk
Arkhangel'sk
NORWAY
SWEDEN
FINLAND
Gor'kiy
Newfoundland
ATLANTIC OCEAN
ICELAND
Reykjavik
Arctic Circle
Leningrad

South Polar Region

ATLANTIC OCEAN
Antarctic Circle
Falkland Is (U.K.)
Novolazarevskaya (U.S.S.R.)
Syowa (Jap.)
ARGENTINA
Tierra del Fuego
Weddell Sea
Dronning Maud Land
Halley (U.K.)
Mawson (Aust.)
Antarctic Peninsula
GREATER ANTARCTICA
Amery Ice Shelf
PACIFIC OCEAN
Ronne Ice Shelf
Shackleton Ice Shelf
Bellingshausen Sea
LESSER ANTARCTICA
South Pole
Transantarctic Mts
Vostok (U.S.S.R.)
Wilkes Land
INDIAN OCEAN
Amundsen Sea
Mt Kirkpatrick ▲ 4528
Ross Ice Shelf
Marie Byrd Land
Scott (N.Z.)
S. Magnetic Pole (1980)
Ross Sea
average minimum extent of sea ice

Other Permanent Stations
1. Arctowski (Pol.)
2. Bellingshausen (U.S.S.R.)
3. Pres. Frei (Ch.)
4. Arturo Prat (Ch.)
5. Petrel (Arg.)
6. Esperanza (Arg.)
7. Grl B.O'Higgins (Ch.)
8. Vco Marambio (Arg.)
9. T.Matienzo (Arg.)
10. Almte Brown (Arg.)
11. Palmer (U.S.)
12. Faraday (U.K.)
13. Grl S.Martin (Arg.)
14. Rothera (U.K.)

1 San Francisco, USA

2 Grand Canyon, USA

3 Diving at Acapulco, Mexico

4 Mayan temple, Mexico

DID YOU KNOW THAT …?

1 The city of San Francisco was almost destroyed by an earthquake in 1906, and there could be another one soon! Right under the city runs the San Andreas fault, where two of the 'plates' which make up the earth's crust slide against one another. When they get jammed together at any point, pressure builds up, until finally they break apart. This causes an earthquake because of the sudden release of so much energy. The longer the plates stay jammed together, the greater the strength of the final earthquake: in 1906, the plates under San Francisco slid 6 m (20 feet) in a few minutes! Some parts of the fault have not moved for years – and scientists think there will be another big earthquake soon.

2 The huge Grand Canyon in Arizona, USA, was gouged out of the rock by the Colorado River. It is 1.6 km (1 mile) deep, a maximum of 29 km (18 miles) wide and no less than 446 km (227 miles) long! The Grand Canyon is still being carved deeper (though very slowly) by the river.

3 At La Questrada, Acapulco, Mexico, divers often swoop 36 m (118 feet) down into the sea! This is the highest dive which people do regularly.

4 The Maya were a tribe who lived in southern Mexico and Guatemala 1400 years ago. They built great cities with stone temples, public buildings and palaces. The picture shows one of their buildings which can be seen today. It was built without help from any modern machinery!

Cattle	Fruit	Wheat	6 Nickel	
Hogs	Sugar cane	Maize	7 Lead	
Bananas	Timber	Minerals	9 Silver	
Citrus fruit	Tobacco	1 Bauxite	11 Uranium	
Cotton	Coal	3 Copper	12 Zinc	
Fish	Oil	5 Iron		

NATURAL VEGETATION/PRODUCTS

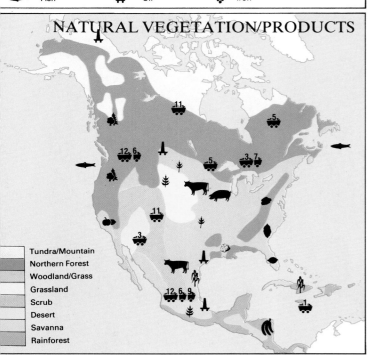

- Tundra/Mountain
- Northern Forest
- Woodland/Grass
- Grassland
- Scrub
- Desert
- Savanna
- Rainforest

POPULATION

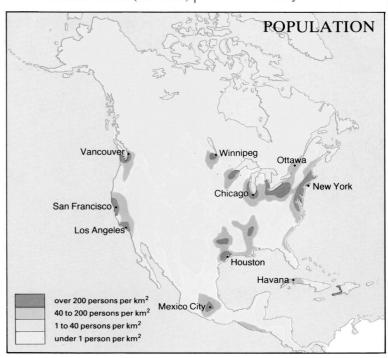

- over 200 persons per km^2
- 40 to 200 persons per km^2
- 1 to 40 persons per km^2
- under 1 person per km^2

CANADA
Area: 9 976 147 sq km (3 851 790 sq miles)
Population: 25 100 000
Capital: Ottawa
Languages: English, French
Currency: Canadian Dollar

CUBA
Area: 114 524 sq km (44 218 sq miles)
Population: 9 900 000
Capital: Havana
Language: Spanish
Currency: Cuban Peso

EL SALVADOR
Area: 20 865 sq km (8056 sq miles)
Population: 4 800 000
Capital: San Salvador
Language: Spanish
Currency: Colon

GUATEMALA
Area: 108 888 sq km (42 042 sq miles)
Population: 8 000 000
Capital: Guatemala
Language: Spanish
Currency: Quetzal

JAMAICA
Area: 11 424 sq km (4411 sq miles)
Population: 2 400 000
Capital: Kingston
Language: English
Currency: Jamaican Dollar

MEXICO
Area: 1 967 180 sq km (759 528 sq miles)
Population: 77 000 000
Capital: Mexico City
Language: Spanish
Currency: Mexican Peso

NICARAGUA
Area: 139 000 sq km (53 668 sq miles)
Population: 2 900 000
Capital: Managua
Language: Spanish
Currency: Cordoba

UNITED STATES OF AMERICA
Area: 9 363 130 sq km (3 615 104 sq miles)
Population: 236 300 000
Capital: Washington
Language: English
Currency: U.S. Dollar

1:15M

200   400   600 km
100   200   300 mls

ARCTIC OCEAN

③ BERING SEA
U.S.S.R.
Bering Str.
BEAUFORT SEA

Norton Sound

Barrow

Prudhoe Bay

Brooks Range

ALASKA (U.S.A.)
Yukon

Fairbanks

Alaska Range

Anchorage

Aleutian Ra.

Wrangell Mts.

Gulf of Alaska

YUKON TERRITORY

Mackenzie Mountains

Whitehorse

Paulatuk

Banks Island

PARRY

Victoria Island

Prince of

NORTH

Great Bear Lake

Mackenzie

Yellowknife

Great Slave Lake

TERRI

K

PACIFIC

Alexander Archipelago

Queen Charlotte Islands

COAST MOUNTAINS

ROCKY

BRITISH

COLUMBIA

MOUNTAINS

Skeena
Kitimat

Vancouver Island

Kamloops

Vancouver

Victoria

Seattle
WASH

Spokane

Portland

CASCADE RANGE

OREGON

WASHINGTON

Nampa

Fraser

Yellowhead Pass

Kicking Horse Pass

Edmonton

Calgary

Medicine Hat

MONTANA

Billings

IDAHO

WYOMING

ALBERTA

Peace

Uranium City

Lake Athabasca

Reindeer Lake

SASKATCHEWAN

Saskatoon

Regina

U. S.

A.

MANIT

Lake Winnipeg

Winnipeg

NORTH DAKOTA

SOUTH DAKOTA

CANADA

N

PACIFIC OCEAN

1:12.5M

① ⓐ BRITISH COLUMBIA
50
Vancouver Island
Vancouver
Seattle WASHINGTON
② Portland Spokane
CASCADE RANGES Mt Ranier 4392
OREGON
Coast Ranges
▲4316 Mt Shasta
40
CALIFORNIA
Reno
San Francisco Sacramento
San Jose Coast Ranges
SIERRA NEVADA
③ Mt Whitney 4418
Death Valley
Las Vegas
Los Angeles San Bernardino
San Diego
PACIFIC OCEAN
BAJA CALIFORNIA
Golfo de California
Hermosillo

ⓑ Edmonton
Calgary
C A N A D A
Saskatoon SASKATCHEWAN ©
Regina
M A N I T
Lake Winnipe
Winn

ROCKY MONTANA
Billings
IDAHO Boise
WYOMING
Great Salt L.
Salt Lake City
NEVADA
UNITED
UTAH
MOUNTAINS
NORTH DAKOTA Bismarck
SOUTH DAKOTA
Missouri
NEBRASKA
Cheyenne
Denver
COLORADO
Colorado Springs
Grand Canyon
Colorado
ARIZONA
Phoenix
NEW MEXICO
Albuquerque
Tucson
El Paso
Chihuahua
SIERRA MADRE OCCIDENTAL
Rio Bravo del Norte
Durango
Mazatlán
M E X I C O
SIERRA MADRE ORIENTAL
Monterrey

Lincoln
KANSAS
Wichita
Tu S
OKLAHOMA
Oklahoma City
Amarillo
Lubbock
T E X A S
Colorado
Dal
San Antonio
Rio Grande

STATES

⑤
160
Kauai
Oahu Honolulu
Molokai
Lanai Maui
155
PACIFIC OCEAN
20N
160
Hawaii
HAWAII 1:6.5M ⓗ
110

20N
100
30
110
120
130

100
200
300
400
500 km
100
200
300 mls

USSR

ALASKA CANADA
Yukon
Fairbanks
Bering
Sea
Anchorage
Whitehorse

Gulf
of
Alaska
Juneau

ALEUTIAN ISLANDS 1:35M **ALASKA**

Thunder
Bay

LAKE SUPERIOR

Duluth

ESOTA

St Paul
eapolis

WISCONSIN

MICHIGAN

LAKE
HURON

Sudbury North
Bay

ONTARIO

Milwaukee

L. MICHIGAN

Toronto

Niagara
Falls

Buffalo

Detroit

LAKE ERIE

Chicago

Toledo Cleveland

INDIANA

OHIO

NEW YORK

Columbus Pittsburgh

Indianapolis Cincinnati

ILLINOIS

Louisville

Lexington

WEST
Charleston

PENNSYLVANIA

Québec

QUEBEC

Montréal

Ottawa
St Lawrence Seaway

MAINE

Fredericton
Saint John

NEW
BRUNSWICK

Gulf of
Saint Lawrence

PRINCE
EDWARD I.

NOVA
SCOTIA

Halifax

Augusta

Montpelier
VERMONT NEW HAMPSHIRE
Concord

Albany MASS. Boston
Hartford Providence
CONN. R.I.

Newark New York
N.J. Philadelphia

Baltimore MD Dover
Washington D.C. Annapolis DEL.

VIRGINIA VIRGINIA
Richmond

St Lawrence

KENTUCKY

Ohio

Kansas
City

Missouri

St Louis

MISSOURI

Ozark Plateaus

Nashville

TENNESSEE

Memphis

Little
Rock

ARKANSAS

Atlanta

Birmingham

MISSISSIPPI ALABAMA GEORGIA

Jackson

LOUISIANA

Baton
Rouge

New Orleans

ouston

GULF OF MEXICO

Raleigh

NORTH CAROLINA

Columbia

SOUTH
CAROLINA

Jacksonville

Tallahassee

FLORIDA

Tampa

Lake
Okeechobee

Miami

Havana
(Habana)

CUBA

Straits of Florida

Andros

Nassau

THE
BAHAMAS

Tropic of Cancer

ATLANTIC

OCEAN

APPALACHIAN MOUNTAINS

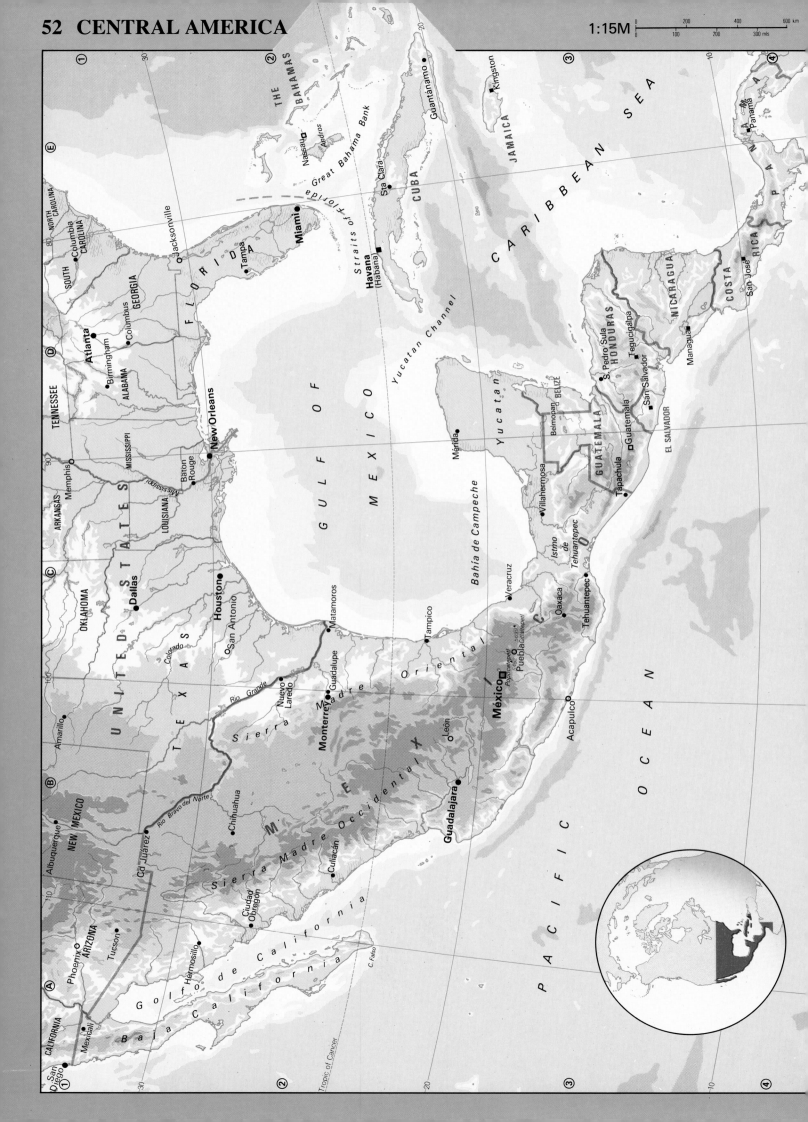

1:15M

① ② ③ ④

200   400   600 km
100   200   300 mils

THE BAHAMAS
Nassau
Andros
Great Bahama Bank

Straits of Florida

Sta Clara
CUBA

Guantánamo

Kingston
JAMAICA

CARIBBEAN SEA

COSTA RICA
San José
Panamá
PANAMA

Miami

Havana
(Habana)

Yucatan Channel

NICARAGUA
Managua

S. Pedro Sula
HONDURAS
Tegucigalpa
San Salvador
EL SALVADOR

Jacksonville
Tampa

FLORIDA

NORTH CAROLINA
Columbia
SOUTH CAROLINA

GEORGIA
Columbus
ALABAMA
Birmingham
Atlanta

TENNESSEE

New Orleans
LOUISIANA
Baton Rouge
MISSISSIPPI

Memphis
ARKANSAS

GULF OF MEXICO

M E X I C O

Mérida

Yucatan

Belmopan
BELIZE
GUATEMALA
Guatemala

Tapachula

Villahermosa
Bahía de Campeche

Veracruz

Istmo de Tehuantepec

Oaxaca
Tehuantepec

OKLAHOMA
Dallas

Houston
San Antonio

Matamoros

Tampico

Popocatépetl
Puebla
Citlaltépetl
México
Acapulco

Guadalupe
Monterrey
Sierra Madre Oriental
Colorado

Rio Grande
Nuevo Laredo

Amarillo

T E X A S

León

Guadalajara

Chihuahua

Sierra Madre Occidental

Culiacán

Ciudad Obregón

Albuquerque
NEW MEXICO
Cd Juárez
Rio Bravo del Norte

U N I T E D   S T A T E S

Phoenix
ARIZONA
Tucson
Hermosillo

C. Falso

Golfo de California

Baja California

Mexicali
San Diego

Tropic of Cancer

P A C I F I C   O C E A N

① ② ③ ④

1:10M

100   200   300   400 km
100
200 mls

Q 1:25 M
DOMINICA
Marigot
Roseau
15°30'

R 1:25 M
BARBADOS
Speightstown
Bridgetown
59°30'

P 1:25 M
ST LUCIA
Castries
Vieux Fort
14
61

N 1:25 M
ST VINCENT
Georgetown
Kingstown
13°15'
61°15'

M 1:25 M
GRENADA
Sauteurs
St George's
12
61°45'

Pt of Spain
San Fernando
Fullarton
Arima
St Joseph
Gulf of Paria
62

Crown Pt
Pt Antonio
Montego Bay
St Ann's Bay
Chapeltown
Portland Pt
Moran

Blue Mts
Kingston
Mandeville
Savanna la Mar
JAMAICA
18
1:25 M

ATLANTIC OCEAN

A T L A N T I C   O C E A N

PUERTO RICO TRENCH

Windward Islands
Tobago
TRINIDAD AND TOBAGO
Bridgetown
BARBADOS
Port of Spain
Trinidad
Carúpano
Maturín
Cd Guayana
Ce Guayana

Leeward Islands
ANTIGUA & BARBUDA
Guadeloupe (Fr.)
Basse Terre
DOMINICA
Roseau
Martinique (Fr.)
Castries
ST LUCIA
Kingstown
ST VINCENT
St George's
GRENADA

St Kitts & Nevis
ST KITTS & NEVIS
Virgin Is (U.S.A & U.K.)

L E S S E R   A N T I L L E S

San Juan
PUERTO RICO (U.S.A.)
Caguas
Ponce
Aguadilla

La Romana
Santiago
Santo Domingo
DOMINICAN REPUBLIC
Cordillera Central
Port-de-Paix
Port-au-Prince
Jacmel
HAITI
Hispaniola

Caicos Is (U.K.)
Acklins
Great Inagua
Andros
THE BAHAMAS
Eleuthera
Great Abaco
Nassau
Tropic of Cancer

Miami
FLORIDA
Straits of Florida
Havana (Habana)
Pinar del Río
Santa Clara
Sagua la Grande
Camagüey
Holguín
Santiago de Cuba
Guantánamo
C U B A

G R E A T E R   A N T I L L E S

CAYMAN TRENCH
Cayman Islands (U.K.)
Montego Bay
Kingston
JAMAICA

C A R I B B E A N   S E A

Caracas
VENEZUELA
Valencia
Barquisimeto
G. de Venezuela
Cabimas
Maracaibo
Valledupar
Lago de Maracaibo
Ciénaga
Barranquilla
Cartagena
Montería
COLOMBIA
Golfo del Darién
Panamá
PANAMA
Panama Canal
Caratasca
Prinzapolca
HONDURAS
NICARAGUA
COSTA RICA
San José

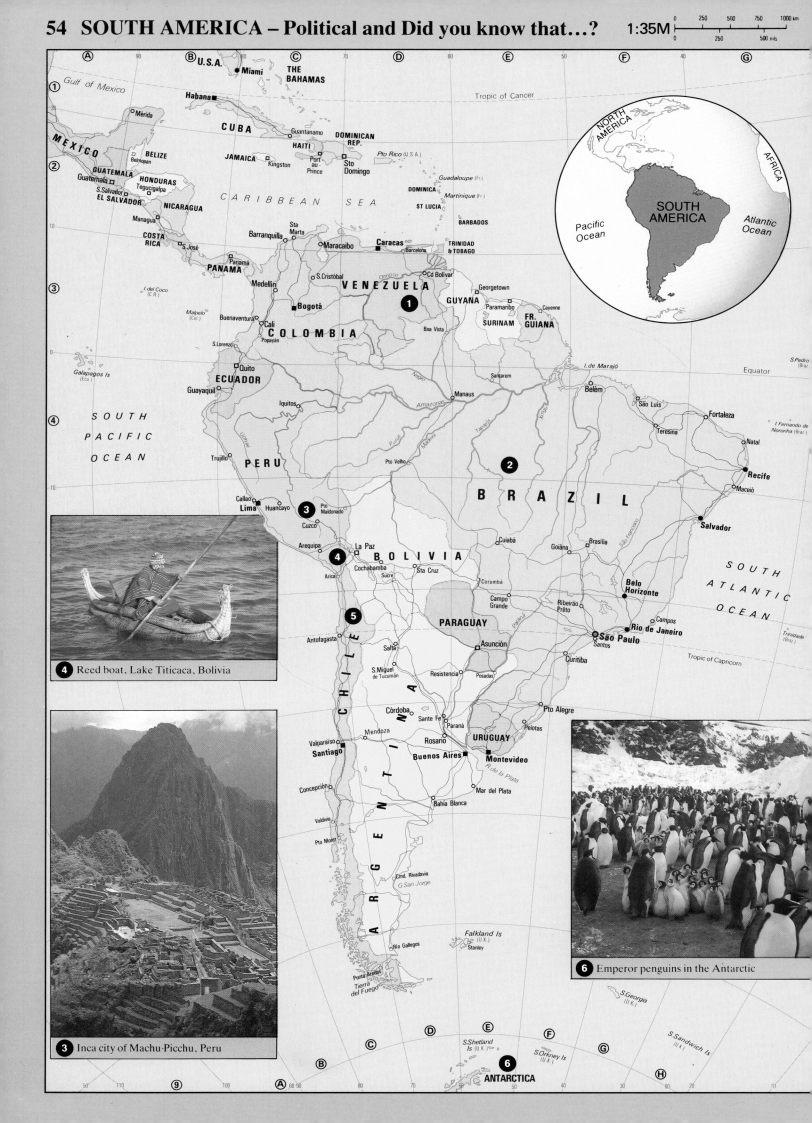

4 Reed boat, Lake Titicaca, Bolivia

3 Inca city of Machu-Picchu, Peru

6 Emperor penguins in the Antarctic

🐄 Cattle	🗼 Oil	3 Copper
🐑 Sheep	🌿 Sugar cane	5 Iron
🫘 Cocoa	🌲 Timber	6 Lead
☕ Coffee	🌾 Wheat	9 Silver
🍎 Fruit	⛏ Minerals	10 Tin
🍌 Bananas	Bauxite	12 Zinc

DID YOU KNOW THAT …?

1 The Angel Falls, Venezuela, are the highest waterfalls in the world, at 979 m (3212 feet).

2 Deforestation is a major problem in South America. About 1 per cent of the total area of forest is lost each year! Often trees are cut down to clear land for agriculture. On hillsides, the soil soon becomes too poor to grow crops and the land is abandoned. Trees cannot grow again, and so soil is eroded away by rain and wind. Trees are also lost when lakes are made for hydro-electric dams; when new towns are built; and as a result of the way people live – they take too much wood for fuel and timber, allow animals to graze on foliage, and light fires which get out of control.

3 In the Andes Mountains, in the north-west of South America, there are ruins of cities built by the Incas. They ruled the Indians in the area 500 years ago. The Incas had well-developed political and religious systems. They built their cities on terraces engineered from the mountain side. The Spanish, the first Europeans to discover these cities, killed the Incas to seize the gold and silver which they had mined, and their cities were abandoned.

4 The highest navigable lake in the world is Lake Titicaca, on the Peru/Bolivia border. It is no less than 3811 m (12 503 feet) above sea level! The local Indian people make boats from bundles of reeds tied together, to use for fishing. The reeds grow around the edge of the lake.

5 Although in the rain forests of the Amazon Basin it rains every day, in the Atacama Desert, Chile, hundreds of years can pass between one rain storm and the next! A storm in 1971 was the first for 400 years. The desert is the driest place in the world.

6 The Emperor Penguin, found in the Antarctic, does not make a nest. Instead, a single egg is carried on top of the male penguin's feet! It is kept warm by a fold of skin which hangs down and covers it. The penguin does not eat during the two months it takes for the egg to hatch out!

NATURAL VEGETATION/ PRODUCTS

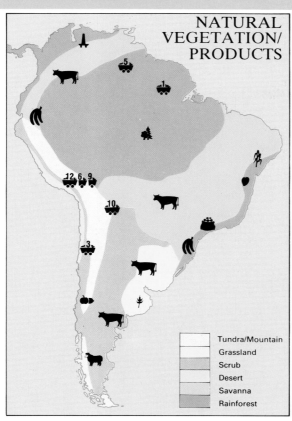

	Tundra/Mountain
	Grassland
	Scrub
	Desert
	Savanna
	Rainforest

POPULATION

	over 200 persons per km²
	40 to 200 persons per km²
	1 to 40 persons per km²
	under 1 person per km²

ARGENTINA

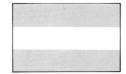

Area: 2 777 815 sq km
(1 072 514 sq miles)
Population: 29 100 000
Capital: Buenos Aires
Language: Spanish
Currency: Argentine Peso

BOLIVIA

Area: 1 098 575 sq km
(424 160 sq miles)
Population: 6 000 000
Capital: La Paz
Languages: Spanish, Aymara, Quechua
Currency: Bolivian Peso

BRAZIL

Area: 8 511 968 sq km
(3 286 471 sq miles)
Population: 134 400 000
Capital: Brasilia
Language: Portuguese
Currency: Cruzeiro

CHILE

Area: 756 943 sq km
(292 256 sq miles)
Population: 11 900 000
Capital: Santiago
Language: Spanish
Currency: Chilean Peso

COLOMBIA

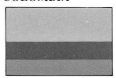

Area: 1 138 907 sq km
(439 732 sq miles)
Population: 28 200 000
Capital: Bogota
Language: Spanish
Currency: Colombian Peso

ECUADOR

Area: 455 502 sq km
(175 869 sq miles)
Population: 9 100 000
Capital: Quito
Language: Spanish
Currency: Sucre

GUYANA

Area: 214 969 sq km
(83 000 sq miles)
Population: 800 000
Capital: Georgetown
Language: English
Currency: Guyanese Dollar

PERU

Area: 1 285 215 sq km
(496 222 sq miles)
Population: 19 200 000
Capital: Lima
Languages: Spanish, Aymara, Quechua
Currency: Sol

VENEZUELA

Area: 912 047 sq km
(352 141 sq miles)
Population: 18 600 000
Capital: Caracas
Language: Spanish
Currency: Bolivar

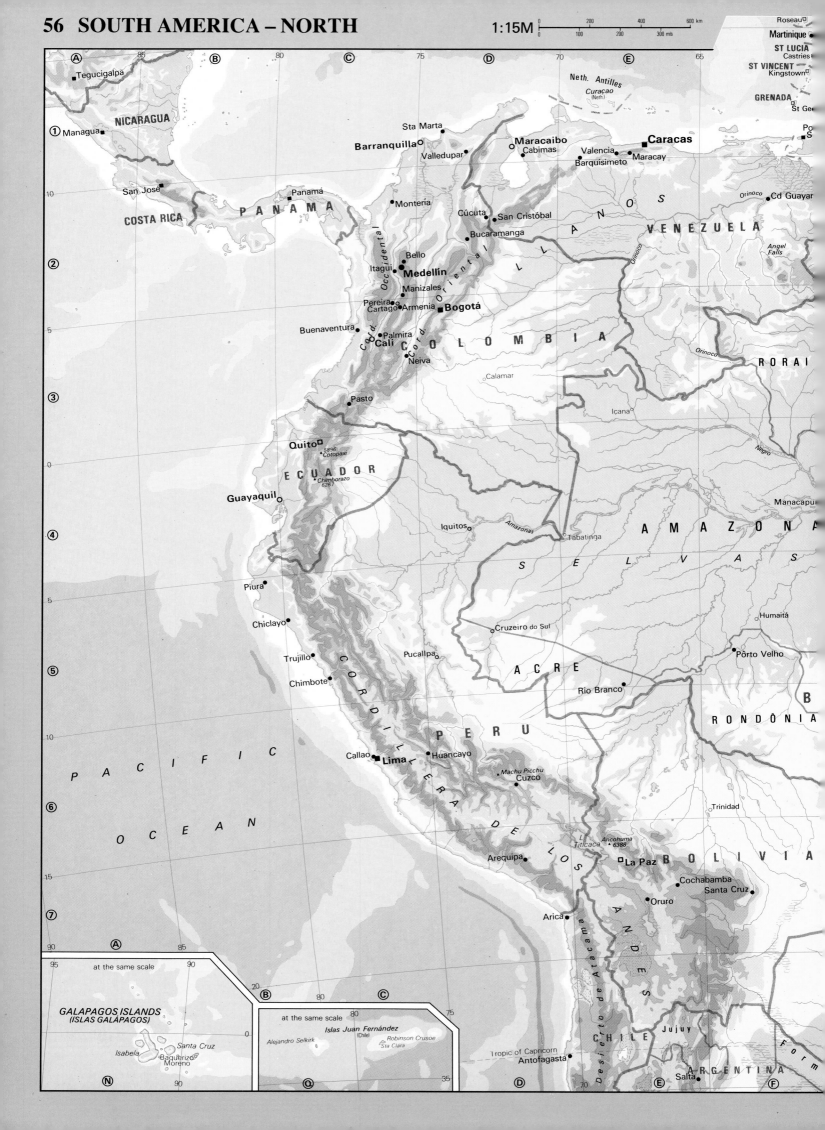

200   400   600 km
100   200   300 mls

Roseau
Martinique
ST LUCIA
Castries
ST VINCENT
Kingstown
GRENADA
St Ge

Tegucigalpa

NICARAGUA
Managua

San José
COSTA RICA

PANAMA

Panamá

Barranquilla
Sta Marta
Valledupar

Maracaibo
Cabimas

Caracas
Valencia
Maracay
Barquisimeto

Neth. Antilles
Curaçao
(Neth)

Monteria
Cúcuta
San Cristóbal
Bucaramanga

VENEZUELA

Orinoco   Cd Guayar

Angel
Falls

Bello
Itagui   Medellín
Manizales
Pereira   Armenia
Cartago   Bogotá
Buenaventura   Palmira
Cali   Neiva

Occidental

Oriental

Cord.

COLOMBIA

L L A N O S

Calamar

R O R A I

Pasto

Orinoco

Icana

Negro

Quito
5896
Cotopaxi

ECUADOR

Chimborazo
6267

Guayaquil

Iquitos

Amazonas

Tabatinga

A M A Z O N A

Manacapu

Piura

S E L V A S

Chiclayo

Cruzeiro do Sul

A C R E

Humaitá

Trujillo
Chimbote

Pucallpa

Pôrto Velho

CORDILLERA

P E R U

Rio Branco

R O N D Ô N I A

B

P A C I F I C

O C E A N

Callao   Lima   Huancayo

Machu Picchu
Cuzco

DE   LOS

Trinidad

Arequipa

L. Titicaca

Ancohuma
6388

La Paz

B O L I V I A

Cochabamba
Santa Cruz

A N D E S

Oruro

Arica

Desierto de Atacama

GALAPAGOS ISLANDS
(ISLAS GALÁPAGOS)

at the same scale

Isabela
Santa Cruz

Baquerizo
Moreno

N

at the same scale

Islas Juan Fernández
(Chile)

Alejandro Selkirk

Robinson Crusoe
Sta Clara

Q

Jujuy

CHILE

Form

Tropic of Capricorn
Antofagasta

Salta

A R G E N T I N A

F

G   55   H   50   J   45   K   40   L   35   M   15

① ② ③ ④ ⑤ ⑥ ⑦ ⑧

BARBADOS
Bridgetown

TRINIDAD
AND
TOBAGO

A T L A N T I C

O C E A N

Georgetown
Paramaribo
Mabaruma
Cayenne

GUYANA   S U R I N A M   FRENCH
GUIANA

ethem

A M A P Á

Macapá

Equator

Amazonas
Belém
Cametá
Santarém
anaus
Itaituba

São Luís

Monção

P A R Á

M A R A N H Ã O
Imperatriz   Teresina
Sobral
Fortaleza (Ceará)

C E A R Á

Mossoró
RIO GRANDE DO NORTE   Natal

Araguaína

P I A U Í

P A R A Í B A
João Pessoa

R   A

Serra do Cachimbo

Caruaru
P E R N A M B U C O   Recife (Pernambuco)
São Francisco

São Félix

Z   I   L

ALAGOAS   Maceió

SERGIPE
Aracajú

Barreiras

B A H I A

Feira de S.

M A T O   G R O S S O

Salvador (Bahia)

Jequié

Planalto de

Mato Grosso

Vitória da
Conquista   Ilhéus

Cáceres

Brasília

G O I Á S

Goiânia

Montes Claros

Paraná

Serra do Espinhaço

Itamaraju

Teófilo Otôni

M A T O   G R O S S O
DO SUL

Uberlândia   M I N A S   G E R A I S
Uberaba

ESPÍRITO

Campo Grande

Belo
Horizonte   Caratinga
Franca   Colatina
SANTO

Dourados   Pres. Prudente   Marília
Limeria

Cachoeiro

S Ã O   P A U L O

Sa de Mantiqueira
Volta
Redonda   Nova Friburgo

P A R A G U A Y

Umuarama
Londrina
Sorocaba   São Paulo   Rio
de Janeiro
Toledo P A R A N Á   São Vicente

Asunción

1:15M

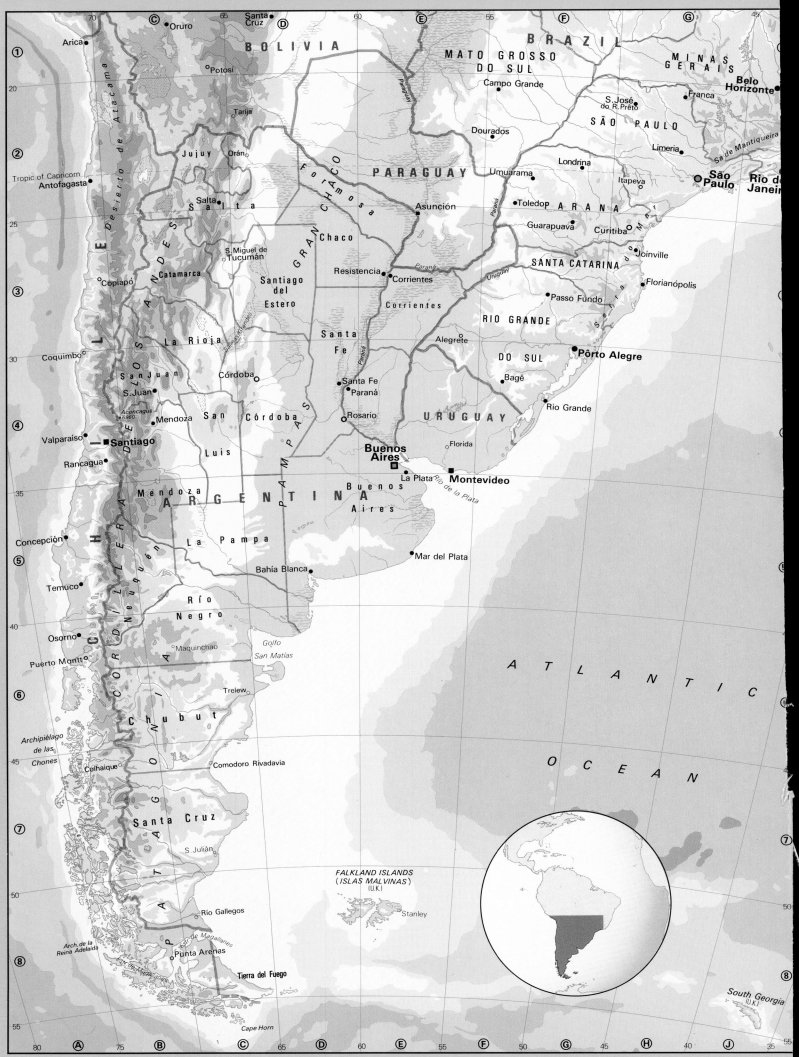

Arica
Oruro
Santa Cruz
BOLIVIA
BRAZIL
MATO GROSSO DO SUL
MINAS GERAIS
Potosí
Campo Grande
S.José do R.Prêto
Franca
Belo Horizonte
Tarija
Dourados
SÃO PAULO
Limeria
Jujuy
Orán
PARAGUAY
Londrina
São Paulo
Rio de Janeiro
Tropic of Capricorn
Antofagasta
Itapeva
Umuarama
Toledop
ARANA
Salta
Asunción
Guarapuava
Curitiba
Chaco
Copiapó
Catamarca
S.Miguel de Tucumán
Resistencia
Corrientes
SANTA CATARINA
Joinville
Florianópolis
Santiago del Estero
Corrientes
Passo Fundo
La Rioja
RIO GRANDE
Coquimbo
Santa Fe
Alegrete
Pôrto Alegre
Córdoba
DO SUL
Bagé
San Juan
S.Juan
Aconcagua 6960
Mendoza
San
Córdoba
Santa Fe
Paraná
Rosario
Rio Grande
Valparaíso
Santiago
Luis
URUGUAY
Rancagua
Buenos Aires
Florida
La Plata
Montevideo
Mendoza
ARGENTINA
Buenos Aires
Concepción
La Pampa
Mar del Plata
Temuco
Bahía Blanca
Osorno
Río Negro
Puerto Montt
Golfo San Matías
Maquinchao
Archipiélago de las Chones
Trelew
ATLANTIC
Chubut
OCEAN
Coihaique
Comodoro Rivadavia
Santa Cruz
S.Julián
FALKLAND ISLANDS (ISLAS MALVINAS) (U.K.)
Stanley
Río Gallegos
Arch. de la Reina Adelaida
Punta Arenas
Tierra del Fuego
South Georgia (U.K.)
Cape Horn

This index helps you to find countries and places shown on the maps in this atlas. Each country or place name is listed in alphabetical order (A to Z), letter by letter. For example, Manchester will come after Madagascar and before Melbourne. After each name, extra information in a shortened form may be given. For example, 'Mts' after the entry 'Grampian' means 'mountains'. The list of abbreviations (shortened words) which follows this introduction tells you what each shortened word description means. The next item in each entry is the name of the country in which the place is. Finally there is a reference number which will look something like this: **16C3**. The first number (before the letter) is the page number (here page 16). The letter and second number lead you to the area on the map on that page where the place can be found. Follow the column labelled with the letter shown (here column C) down from the top of the page. Follow the row with the same number (here row 3) in from the side of the page. Where the column and row meet is the part of the map where you will find the place you looked up (**16C3** is the reference for London, England). Practise looking up a few places in the index and on the maps. Try to find Sydney, Australia; New York, U.S.A.; Paris, France.

Arch	Archipelago	O	Ocean
B	Bay	P	Pass
C	Cape	Pass	Passage
Chan	Channel	Pen	Peninsula
Des	Desert	Plat	Plateau
Gl	Glacier	Pt	Point
G. of	Gulf of	Res	Reservoir
H(s)	Hills(s)	R	River
I(s)	Islands(s)	S	Sea
Lg	Lagoon	Sd	Sound
L	Lake	Str	Strait
Mt(s)	Mountain(s)	V	Valley

A

Abādān *Iran*	41A4
Abéché *Chad*	24C2
Aberdeen *Scotland*	16C2
Abidjan *Ivory Coast*	23B4
Abū Dhabi *U.A.E.*	38P3
Acapulco *Mexico*	52C3
Accra *Ghana*	23B4
Acklins, I *Caribbean*	53C2
Aconcagua, Mt *Chile*	58B4
Acre, State *Brazil*	56D5
Addis Ababa *Ethiopia*	24D3
Adelaide *Australia*	42C4
Aden = ('Adan) *S. Yemen*	38C4
Aden, G. of *Yemen/Somalia*	38C4
Adriatic, Sea *Italy/Yugos*	18C2
Afghanistan, Republic *Asia*	26E4
Āgra *India*	39F3
Aguadilla *Puerto Rico*	53D3
Ahmadābād *India*	39F3
Ahvāz *Iran*	41E3
Ajaccio *Corsica*	18B2
Akita *Japan*	37E4
Aktyubinsk *USSR*	32G4
Akureyri *Iceland*	13B1
Alabama, State *USA*	51E3
Alagoas, State *Brazil*	57L5
Alaska, G. of *USA*	48D4
Alaska, State *USA*	48C3
Alaska Range, Mts *USA*	48C3
Albacete *Spain*	20B2
Albania, Republic *Europe*	11H4
Albany *USA*	51F2
Alberta, Province *Canada*	48G4
Alborg *Denmark*	14B1
Al Bū Kamāl *Syria*	41D3
Albuquerque *USA*	50C3
Alegrete *Brazil*	58E3
Aleutian Range, Mts *USA*	48C4
Alexandria *Egypt*	41A3
Algeria, Republic *N. Africa*	21E5
Algiers = (Alger) *Algeria*	20C2
Al Hadithah *Iraq*	41D3
Al Hudaydah *Yemen*	24E2
Alicante *Spain*	20B2
Alice Springs *Australia*	42C3
Al 'Isawiyah *Saudi Arabia*	41C3
Al Jālāmid *Saudi Arabia*	41D3
Al Lādhiqīyah *Syria*	41C2
Allāhabad *India*	39G3
Alma-Ata *USSR*	39F1
Al Manāmah *Bahrain*	38D3
Al Mudawwara *Jordan*	41C4
Alpi Dolomitiche, Mts *Italy*	18C1
Alps, Mts *Europe*	18B1

Altai, Mts *Mongolia*	32K5
Altay, Mts *USSR*	32K4
Amapá, State *Brazil*	57H3
Amarillo *USA*	50C3
Amazonas, R *Brazil*	57H4
Amazonas, State *Brazil*	56E4
Ambarchik *USSR*	45C7
Ambon *Indonesia*	42B1
American Samoa, Is *Pacific O.*	43H2
Amery Ice Shelf *Antarctica*	45G10
Amman *Jordan*	41C3
Amsterdam *Netherlands*	14A2
Amundsen, S *Antarctica*	45F4
Amur, R *USSR*	33P4
Anchorage *USA*	48D3
Ancohuma, Mt *Bolivia*	56E7
Ancona *Italy*	18C2
Andorra, Principality *S.W. Europe*	20C1
Andorra-La-Vella *Andorra*	20C1
Angmagssalik *Greenland*	49P3
Angola, Republic *Africa*	21F9
Ankara *Turkey*	41B2
'Annaba *Algeria*	23C1
An Najaf *Iraq*	41D3
Annapolis *USA*	51F3
An Nāsirīyah *Iraq*	41E3
Anshan *China*	36E1
Antananarivo *Madagascar*	25E5
Antarctic, Pen *Antarctica*	45G3
Antarctic Circle *Antarctica*	45G1
Antigua and Barbuda, Is *Caribbean*	53E3
Antofagasta *Chile*	58B2
Antwerp *Belgium*	17C1
Apia *W. Samoa*	43H2
Appalachian, Mts *USA*	51E3
Appennines, Mts *Italy*	18C2
Arabian, S *Asia/Arabian Peninsula*	38E4
Arad *Romania*	15E3
Arafura, S *Indonesia/Australia*	42D1
Araguaína *Brazil*	57J5
Arbīl *Iraq*	41D2
Arctic Circle	45C1
Arctic, Ocean *N. Europe*	32
Ardabīl *Iran*	41E2
Arequippa *Peru*	56D7
Argentina, Republic *S. America*	54D7
Århus *Denmark*	13G7
Arica *Chile*	58B1
Arizona, State *USA*	50B3
Arkansas, State *USA*	51D3

Arkhangel'sk *USSR*	32F3
Armenia *Colombia*	56C3
Ar Rutbah *Iraq*	41D3
Asahikawa *Japan*	37E3
Ashkhabad *USSR*	38D2
Asmara *Ethiopia*	24D2
Astrakhan' *USSR*	32F5
Asunción *Paraguay*	58E3
Aswân *Egypt*	38B3
Atbara *Sudan*	24D2
Athabasca, L *Canada*	48H4
Athens = (Athinai) *Greece*	19E3
Atlanta *USA*	51E3
Atlantic, O	10C3
Auckland *New Zealand*	44B1
Augusta *USA*	51G2
Australia, Commonwealth Nation *S.W. Pacific*	27H7
Austria, Federal Republic *Europe*	10G4
Ayers Rock *Australia*	42C3
Azores, Islands *Atlantic O.*	23A1

B

Badajoz *Spain*	20A2
Baden-Württemburg, State *W. Germany*	14B3
Baffin, B *Greenland/Canada*	49M2
Baffin, I *Canada*	49L3
Bagé *Brazil*	58F4
Baghdād *Iraq*	41D3
Bahamas, The, Is *Caribbean*	51F4
Bahia, State *Brazil*	57K6
Bahía Blanca *Argentina*	58D5
Bahia de Campeche, B *Mexico*	52C2
Bahrain, Sheikdom *Arabian Peninsula*	38D3
Baja California, State *Mexico*	50B4
Baku *USSR*	32F5
Balearic, Is *Spain*	20C2
Balikpapan *Indonesia*	42A1
Baltic, S *N. Europe*	13H7
Baltimore *USA*	51F3
Bamako *Mali*	23B3
Banda Aceh *Indonesia*	40B4
Bandung *Indonesia*	35D7
Bangalore *India*	39F4
Bangassou *C.A.R.*	24C3
Bangkok *Thailand*	40C3
Bangladesh, Republic *Asia*	26F4
Bangui *C.A.R.*	24B3
Ban Me Thuot *Vietnam*	40D3
Banjarmasin *Indonesia*	35E7
Banjul *The Gambia*	23A3
Banks, I *Canada*	48F2
Ban Me Thuot *Vietnam*	40D3
Baotou *China*	36C1
Barbados, I *Caribbean*	53F4
Barbuda, I *Caribbean*	53F4
Barcelona *Spain*	20C1
Barents, S *USSR*	32D2
Bari *Italy*	18D2
Barnaul *USSR*	32K4
Barquisimeto *Venezuela*	56E1
Barranquilla *Colombia*	56D1
Basel *Switzerland*	18B1
Basra *Iraq*	41E3
Basse Terre *Guadeloupe*	53E3
Bass Strait *Australia*	42D4
Bata *Equat. Guinea*	24A3
Batna *Algeria*	23C1
Batumi *USSR*	41D1
Beaufort, S *Canada*	45B5
Béchar *Algeria*	23B1
Beersheba *Israel*	41B3
Beirut *Lebanon*	41C3
Belém *Brazil*	57J4
Belfast *N. Ireland*	16B3
Belgium, Kingdom *N.W. Europe*	10F3
Belgrade = (Beograd) *Yugoslavia*	19E2
Belize, Republic *C. America*	52D3
Bellingshausen, S *Antarctica*	45G3
Bello *Colombia*	56C2
Belo Horizonte *Brazil*	57K7
Beloye More, S *USSR*	32E3
Bengal, B. of *Asia*	39G4
Benin, Republic *Africa*	21E7

Benin City *Nigeria*	23C4
Benxi *China*	36E1
Berbera *Somalia*	24E2
Bergen *Norway*	13F6
Bering, S *USSR/USA*	33T3
Bering, Str *USSR/USA*	45C6
Berlin *Germany*	14C2
Bern *Switzerland*	18B1
Bhutan, Kingdom *Asia*	26F4
Bialystok *Poland*	15E2
Bight of Benin, B *W. Africa*	23C4
Bight of Biafra, B *Cameroon*	23C4
Bilbao *Spain*	20B1
Billings *USA*	50C2
Birmingham *England*	16C3
Birmingham *USA*	51E3
Bir Moghrein *Mauritania*	23A2
Biscay, B *France/Spain*	17A2
Bissau *Guinea Bissau*	23A3
Black, S *USSR/Europe*	32E5
Black Volta, R *Burkina*	23B3
Blagoveshchensk *USSR*	33O4
Blanc, Mt *France/Italy*	17D2
Blantyre *Malawi*	25D5
Bloemfontein *S. Africa*	25C6
Blue, Mts *Jamaica*	53J1
Bobo Dioulasso *Burkina*	23B3
Bobruysk *USSR*	15F2
Bodø *Norway*	13G5
Bogotá *Colombia*	56D3
Boise *USA*	50B2
Bolgatanga *Ghana*	23B3
Bolivia, Republic *S. America*	54D5
Bologna *Italy*	17E3
Bombay *India*	39F4
Bonn *W. Germany*	14B2
Bordeaux *France*	17B3
Borneo, I *Malaysia/Indonesia*	35E6
Bornholm, I *Denmark*	13G7
Bosporus, Sd *Turkey*	19F2
Boston *USA*	51F2
Bothnia, G. of *Sweden/Finland*	13H6
Botswana, Republic *Africa*	21G10
Bouaké *Ivory Coast*	23B4
Boulogne *France*	17C1
Brahmaputra, R *India*	39H3
Brasilia *Brazil*	57J7
Bratsk *USSR*	33M4
Brazil, Republic *S. America*	54E4
Brazzaville *Congo*	24B4
Bremen *W. Germany*	14B2
Brenner, P *Austria/Italy*	14C3
Breslau *Poland*	14D2
Brest *France*	17B2
Bridgetown *Barbados*	53F4
Brisbane *Australia*	43E3
Bristol *England*	16C3
British Columbia, Province *Canada*	48F4
Brooks Range, Mts *USA*	48C3
Brunei, Sultanate *S.E. Asia*	35E6
Brussels = (Brüssel/Bruxelles) *Belgium*	14A2
Bryansk *USSR*	32E4
Bucaramanga *Colombia*	56D2
Bucharest = (Bucuresti) *Romania*	19F2
Budapest *Hungary*	15D3
Buenaventura *Colombia*	56C3
Buenos Aires *Argentina*	58E4
Buenos Aires, State *Argentina*	58E5
Buffalo *USA*	51F2
Bujumbura *Burundi*	24C4
Bukavu *Zaïre*	24C4
Bulawayo *Zimbabwe*	25C6
Bulgaria, Republic *Europe*	11H4
Burgas *Bulgaria*	38A1
Burgos *Spain*	20B1
Burkina, Republic *Africa*	21F8
Burma, Republic *Asia*	26F4
Burundi, Republic *Africa*	21G8

C

Cabimas *Venezuela*	56D1
Cabinda, Province *Angola*	24B4
Cáceres *Brazil*	57G7
Cachoeiro de Itapemirim *Brazil*	57K8